Never Say Die

A Zombie Time Loop Story

A Young Adult Novel

Kimberly Gould

Never Say Die

A Zombie Time Loop Story

Second Edition

April 2017

ISBN: 978-1-926514-85-7,

978-1-926514-86-4

Published by eBTT YA Generations Books

Dedication

For Delilah, the future is yours.

ACKNOWLEDGEMENTS

A big thank you goes to Jay Donovan for supporting my endeavor and lending a little military and gun know-how to Cassandra.
To Angela Rackard-Campbell for her editing, and the biggest to my new publisher, eBTT YA Generations Books, for raising this story from the dead.

Chapter One

I STAND ready, my guard up. I know the attack could come from either side, but will most likely come from behind. They love biting into the back of a neck, breaking it if possible, that way the kill stays fresh while they feed. Disgusting creatures. I'm not about to have my blood taint the snow. However, I face the building, watching for my best friend and partner to emerge.

It's not bright, exposing my neck, but without guns, luring them in close is the only sure way to kill them. They aren't terribly cautious but can recognize a kid with a rifle or Glock. I have neither anymore.

Why didn't we bring more ammunition? I mean really, we knew what we were in for when we got outside the fence. Sometimes we really are just a bunch of stupid kids. I'm definitely finding reloads before we head back. This city is hardly stripped at all. We aren't here for supplies, but people.

The graffiti on the wall is fresh. "We are inside." Smart kids. The meat sacks don't have enough sense to read, and even if they do make out the words, they don't understand. Other kids, like Heph and me, we can read just fine.

I shiver slightly in the cold, but the tension I have coiled in muscles, ready to pounce, is keeping me warm. The icy wind ruffles my short spiky hair, and I add hats and scarves to the shopping list when we have the kids and can raid the town. What is taking Heph so long, anyway? Get the kids and get out.

Crunch.

I whirl to meet my opponent, blade raised.

The brainless meat sack is fast and ugly as sin, slathered in crap and dirt, but he'll be much prettier without that head. His black-red blood stains the snow, not mine, and I turn for his friend, adding another kill to my tally. Heph will be pissed when I pass him again.

Heph saved me, literally. I was a crying, scared, running wreck when he took me under his wing, taught me to fight, to shoot, to hot wire a car, break into a building. His total kills topped mine for a long time, but I've learned and I'm faster than he is. My score grew with experience, slowly matching and overtaking his death toll. I was in the lead when we left Freetown, but he got to count all the bodies he mowed down in the truck. Hardly fair. This mob should be enough to push me over again.

My cockiness is my demise. I see something red in the distance as a monster bites into the side of my neck and I scream in pain and rage. My glasses are knocked from my head and I fall to my knees, everything going dark. I can't die, there are too many people counting on me, too much to do. I don't even know if Heph got the kids out.

***

My legs are wet. Why are my legs wet? I smell salt, and feel a breeze. Are there breezes in hell? I suppose I could be in heaven, but I doubt they'd take me. I'm pretty sure I broke every rule there ever was in a bid to survive. Opening my eyes, I prepare for the worst.

Wait a minute. I've been here before, months ago, before the incident, before the virus turned most of us into monsters. Why am I here?

I start to get up and realize I'm wearing the same dress I wore a lifetime ago, and my dark hair is long, hanging in waves over my shoulder. I'm also wearing my contact lenses. How long since I had a pair of those? This is some dream. Heading back down the path that had brought me here so long ago, I find my parents — my dead parents.

“Mom?” I ask, choking on the word. “Dad?” I run to them and hug my mother tightly. Maybe I am in heaven.

“Cassy? What’s wrong, honey? Weren’t you having fun?” she asks, smoothing my hair.

“Fun?” I ask, incredulous. “Yeah, lots of fun. It’s great watching monsters tear apart everyone you love.” The tears that started at the sight of my parents multiply and roll down my cheeks. “Really riotous.”

“Cassy?” my father asks in a serious tone. His blue eyes are as solid as his voice. “Are you okay?”

“No, I’m not okay. I’m obviously dead.”

My parents look at each other and I can see the questions they’re asking without speaking. What has gotten into her?

“I’m not insane,” I argue, pulling away from them. “This place stinks.” I storm off wondering why, if this is heaven, they are acting so oddly?

“Cassy, wait!” My mom chases after me, her brown curls bouncing more than mine. They’re shorter, the way my hair used to be. "Talk to us. Tell us what happened."

"You both died, okay? You were infected and turned into...them." My voice cracks, and I stomp even harder. My stupid hair will not stay out of my mouth. "Bleh, and why give me back this?" I fight my hair into a knot.

"You love your hair, honey. You've been growing it out since you were four." My mother tugs on a lock. She's right. It was my pride and joy, the way the light bounced off it, giving highlights and redness. It has a gentle wave that is neither too curly nor stick straight. It gives it volume off the top of my head, looking full and luxurious. My friends always told me I should model in shampoo commercials. However…

"Yeah, well, it's a pain in the ass when you don't have reliable water and it gets caught in everything." Absolutely true. After pulling most of a bush out of it the first night running from my rabid parents, I tamed it back. Then I got thrown into a pool of blood and wasn't able to wash for two days. "That's why I cut it off six months ago."

"Six months ago you were asking Julie to braid your hair," my mother's brow is knit in confusion and I'm starting to feel the same.

"Yeah, if this really was July of 'fifteen." 2015, the year everything ended. 2016, the year those of us left tried to make a beginning.

"But…it is." The sun gleams off the top of my father's head and I wonder why heaven wouldn't give him back his hair. "You were just walking into the surf and then sat on the shore. You were so happy a moment ago." He rubs my shoulder. He's a full seven inches taller than me and his strength is always reassuring. Of course, at his words I don't need reassurance, I need to be grounded. It can't be true, can it?

"Shut up." My mouth sags a little. "It's really July tenth? Manson is still in business? There haven't been any...accidents?" I ask, trying to lead them.

"No honey. Manson? Since when are you interested in drug companies?" I can tell he thinks I'm on the drugs.

"Just since they bred a super virus," I mumble. "It's really July tenth and I really just graduated a couple weeks ago?"

"Yes, Cassy. Your tassel is still hanging from the mirror of the car."

"We still have the old Ford!" I remember how important a vehicle that was simple to fix became. The Taurus isn't here, we came in the Caravan, but it's waiting at home. "I can do something! Maybe I can stop the whole damn thing." I give each of my parents another hug, digging in Dad's pocket for his keys. "Call a cab. I'm taking the car. Trust me. Bye!"

"Cassy? Cassy!" My mother's shout is lost behind me as my hair falls out of its knot. My legs tangle in my skirt and I yank it higher, hoping there's a knife or scissors in the glove box. I need to lose this hair and then I need to kill a very bad doctor, hopefully before he breeds the end of mankind.

Jumping behind the wheel of the Caravan, my eye catches the bundle of threads dangling from the rear-view mirror with a silver fifteen attached.

"Trippy." I touch the blue and green gingerly. It's almost as trippy as my hair and this dress. I haven't worn anything like this in ages. Most of us wear some version of army fatigues. I turn the ignition and pull away. Getting on the interstate, I try to remember how far I have to go. Home is so much closer to ground zero, Albuquerque. We live in Gallup, just a quick drive away, but it will take hours to get there from Monterey, this beach. I'll probably pull in around eight or nine. Should I stop at the house? Is there anything there I need?

Not really. Heph, but he can't help me right now. It doesn't take two of us to kill one man.

Death has become such a regular part of my life and the fact Evans isn't a meat sack yet doesn't deter me one bit. He's the source of the virus, therefore, he must be stopped before he creates it. Easiest way? Remove him, just like I've been removing meat sacks for months.

Easiest way, how should I kill him? For the first time, I realize that I could be arrested, I could go to jail. There were no authorities where I came from. There was us and death, pretty simple choice. Rather, no choice. I wouldn't accept death.

I laugh at that thought; I wouldn't accept death, and I'm not dead! How funny is that? Pouring on a little more speed, I start to get into the flow of traffic, weaving through it. It's familiar, even though I haven't experienced in a long time.

Can I kill Evans without getting caught? I could use a blade, maybe one from his own house. They might be able to trace it to me, but nothing connects me to him. I wouldn't even know his name except that we began using it as a curse word.

"For Evans sake!"

"Pulling an Evans, are you?"

"Peter C. Evans!"

Peter C. Evans, Dr. Evans. I know little more than his name and his place at the beginning of the end of existence.

He worked for Manson, in their lab in Albuquerque, as a bioengineer. Designing fighter viruses and bacteria, his breakthrough came breeding a bug to kill the bad bugs. Sounded good in theory, but instead of attacking enemy cells, it attacks the brain, leaving an animal that knows only one thing: hunger.

None of that tells me where he lives or what hours he works. I pull my Mom's phone out of the glove box and start searching online. God, how nice is it to have internet? Now that I know where he lives, I can just wait for him to come home.

Flying through my hometown gives me a twinge of homesickness and regret. It will burn down in a few weeks. Adults living alone will leave things turned on when the virus claims them and the firemen that would normally help will be busy eating one another. If they head to fires, it'll be with a taste for cooked meat. Oddly enough, it will be a blessing. Those of us who still have brains will be able to group while the meat sacks flee or burn.

The sun is just setting when I hit Albuquerque's limits. I get lost twice trying to find the doctor's house. A little boy, probably four, is playing on the front lawn. He still has rings of baby fat on his arms and legs and his cheeks are full. His blonde hair is sparse, like it's still growing in, and sticks up at odd angles. His mother comes to stand on the front step and call him into the house.

Four. Few younger than six will survive. This boy will probably be eaten by the mother that feeds him.

Why didn't I consider he might have a family? Why did I assume he was alone? I'm so wrapped up in consideration for those bystanders that I almost miss him pulling into his driveway. He isn't wearing the lab coat that he has on in every picture I've seen, but I recognize his slicked back brown hair and plastic rimmed glasses.

"Peter Evans," I murmur, before restarting the engine and pulling away.

I find a nearby convenience store and pick up a pair of scissors. This hair will only get tangled as I try to sneak into the house. It would be nice to have some other clothes, but most of the actual shops have already closed for the night. Instead, I dig around the back of the van in Dad's bag and find one of his shirts—dark green. It'll do. Better than my white skin. I pull it on over the dress.

Behind the store, I open the packaging for the scissors and begin sawing through my hair. If this works, I'll be able to get it straightened. If not, I won't care what my hair looks like anyway. I do look wistfully at the locks on the pavement. Already my head feels lighter and clearer. Feeling better prepared, I return to the Evans' house.

There's no signage for a burglar alarm, but I'm betting they have one. I could probably disarm it, but it's safer to evade it. I wait in the backyard, peering into the kitchen. Mrs. Evans is moving around and when her back is turned, I slip in the back door and hide behind the coat rack.

This is ridiculous. My legs are obvious, only my torso hidden by the coats. Mrs. Evans finishes her clean up and turns off the light to my relief. She didn't look my way, apparently. Feeling safer in the dark, I slip through the kitchen and choose a knife from the block. The blade reflects the light from a neighbor's back porch and I tuck it in my elbow by reflex. The meat sacks are stupid, but like any other animal, they're attention is grabbed by shiny things. Even after all other intelligence is gone, that instinct remains.

Pressing myself flat to the wall, I peek around the corner to see the Evans watching television. The stairway is also dark and I climb quietly toward the light at the top. It isn't a bright light, muted by some sort of shade.

The room is blue with clouds painted on the walls. The light is a single bulb plugged into the wall, a night light. The boy is asleep atop his covers, holding his teddy bear.

“I hope you live this time,” I tell him in a whisper.

I hear a creak from downstairs and begin ducking through doors, searching for the master bedroom. When I find it, I dive under the bed, holding my breath. I let it out in soft quick puffs, trying to even it out as quietly as possible.

I cringe at the loud kissing going on over my head and pray they aren’t going to have sex tonight. I do not want to listen to that. I’m in luck, and after a few more kisses they both fall silent.

Continuing to hide under the bed, I count to a thousand. Over five minutes, less than ten. It should be enough for them to be drowsy, if not asleep. It will have to be because I can’t hold myself back any longer. Knowing what is coming, what this man will make, I am determined to stop him. Rolling out, I crouch beside the bed, looking up. I’m on the right side, his side. Dr. Evans is snoring just inches from my nose.

He looks peaceful, like just an ordinary guy, not a man about to destroy the world.

After testing the edge of the knife quickly, I pull it across his throat, pressing hard. His eyes open, but he can only gurgle. I've cut deep and his windpipe isn't working any more. His wife snuffs and turns while he scrabbles to grab me.

Stepping back, he's easy to evade. "You can't be allowed to kill us all." He has enough strength left to grab his wife, waking her. I run for the stairs just as she screams. The boy is there, blonde hair sticking up on one side.

"Who are you?" he asks.

I don't have a witty answer and push past him down the stairs. The burglar alarm goes off now, but I've already dropped the knife on the lawn and am peeling away in the Caravan, headed home. They might identify me, but I doubt they will.

Before I get home, I have to pull over on the highway. My arms and legs tremble with the knowledge of what I've done. I've killed hundreds of meat sacks—243 to be exact—but never a conscious person. My stomach, roiling since his thinking human eyes found mine, empties into the ditch. I pull off Dad's shirt and wipe the blood from my hands, dropping it in the ditch as well.

Sitting against the rear tire of the Caravan, I laugh hysterically. I did it. I saved the human race.

Chapter Two

"Cassandra! Cassandra, wake up!"

My mother's voice reaches me through the fog clouding my head. My mother's voice. My living, breathing mother. I smile as I stretch. "Yes?"

"Don't you 'yes' me, miss. Where did you go last night? Do you have any idea how much tickets home cost us? Why is there blood on the steering wheel?"

Blood on the wheel? Damn, I was sloppier than I thought.

The mattress sags as my mother sits next to me. The worry line in the middle of her forehead is deep, only slightly covered by her brown bangs. "Is something wrong, honey? This isn't like you. I mean, your hair." Mom often flips like this. She starts mad as hell and then, after a few questions, turns soft and tries to get me or Dad to talk. She figures if we're defensive, it's for a reason and she wants to know what it is. Well, there is a very good reason, but she will never believe it.

I yawn and pause in the process of finger-combing the crooked locks. "Oh yeah, about that. Think I can get it straightened?"

"What's wrong?" she repeats, her hazel eyes serious and intent. There's a spark of anger there too. I'm not surprised she's pissed at me, but right now she's more worried there is something really wrong. In fact, everything is perfect from my point of view.

Is there anything I can offer? Any small grain of truth she might be able to accept? Nope. "Nothing."

"Cassy, you know you can tell us anything. We'll do anything to help."

Obviously, she would never guess what I had been doing, but what is her guess? That I was out at some rave last night? "Really Mom, everything is fine now, better than fine." I throw back my pink comforter and notice I'm still in the dress from yesterday. It's a little crusty where the sea water dried.

"You'd tell us if something was wrong?"

"Yes Mom. God. I'm fine. I just had to take care of something last night, something time sensitive."

"Okay, but the price of the tickets is coming out of your paycheck, and you shouldn't make plans to go anywhere but work." Mom's also fair. That's going to be most of my summer wages, assuming I go to work. I'm feeling a little too satisfied with myself and my actions to want to go scoop ice cream every other night for two months.

"Sure. Fine." I guess I'll have to work, and it is still worth every penny.

She hugs me and reluctantly leaves the room. I stretch onto my toes and pull off the sarong. Stopping at a mirror, I smile at my reflection. Am I glowing? It feels like it. My brown eyes definitely sparkle. It's going to be a good day. "I'm calling Heph!" I sing to myself as I don a robe and head for a shower, a really hot shower. It seems ages since I've had one.

"Who's Heph?" my father asks from down the hall.

"A boy," I answer loudly. "Not one I saw last night."

"Good!" he shouts back. It's followed by some grumbling that would probably be threatening if I was close enough to hear.

Flopping on my bed in a towel, I spy my clock. Either Mom and Dad got back late, or they let me sleep in. It's almost noon. I find my phone and dial the number I remember from months ago.

"Hello?"

"Heph?"

"One of, but since you've called Jonah's phone, I'm guessing you don't want to talk to me."

"Who is it?" I hear faintly in the background.

"I don't know, some girl."

The woman's voice is louder when I hear it next. "Jonah is grounded. He won't be able to take any calls until Friday."

"Oh, I see. I'll call back later." I look at my phone in wonder as I disconnect. Grounded? The concept seems foreign to me, mostly because I haven't been grounded since I was thirteen, but also because I came from a place where there was no one to ground us. If anything we grounded ourselves, locking ourselves in a compound for safety. Grounded.

Shaking my head, I toss the phone aside before pulling on clothes and glasses. Even though I haven't had a wardrobe in six months, I don't really care what I put on. All of it is fashionable, make that nearly impractical. A v-neck tee and shorts. They each hug my hips and chest to show off my fully developed curves. My boobs aren't huge, but the boys appreciate what I have. They would get shredded wearing something like this. I lean into the mirror looking at the skin above my breasts. My chest had been shredded when I first ran, but there are no white scars now. Going back in time is pretty cool.

"I thought she was kidding," my dad says as I round the corner in search of breakfast. He looks up from the paper spread over the table to do a double take. "You really cut your hair." He has today off as part of our holiday, likely the reason I got to sleep in—they weren't up themselves.

"Yeah? So?"

"And you're wearing your glasses."

I shrug. "Didn't feel like poking myself in the eye today."

"I kinda like your hair. You are getting it fixed?" One furry eyebrow climbs toward his long-gone hairline. What he lacks on top, Dad makes up for in his eyebrows and beard, both dark with flecks of grey.

I laugh. "It's nice but needs to be fixed?"

"Well, it's obviously rough, but I like it around your face."

I push a lock behind an ear. "Thanks. I think I'm going to keep it short."

He slurps from his mug. "So, what happened yesterday?"

"Nothing," I say with a sigh, flopping into a chair with an orange. "I just forgot about something I had to do."

"Something you had to do in Albuquerque."

"What?"

"The mileage on the Caravan. You didn't come straight home. I just guessed, since you mentioned Manson yesterday, where you'd gone. Then there's the blood. What's going on, Cassy?" He regards me over his own glasses, blue eyes serious.

I take a deep breath. He isn't going to believe me anyway. I don't quite believe it yet. "I had to stop a doctor from making something that would destroy everyone."

He waits, but I don't have anything else to tell him. "Let me know when you have some details to make that one believable."

I slouch in my chair. Dad does a lot of writing in his job, non-fiction, but he loves to turn everything into a story. "I will," I grumble.

A few hours later, I'm sitting in a salon. Everything I do today just exaggerates how different things are. A place like this didn't exist where I came from. No one wasted time on how they looked. Staying warm — yes. Keeping clean enough that you didn't get sick — yes. Painting your nails — God, no. Who has time for that? I look at my nails and notice how clean they are, how long. I'd cut them to the quick every week. Who wanted to think about what got stuck under them?

"Oh. My. God."

"Just fix it," I tell the stylist coldly. "I want it to--I don't know--wing out here." I made a motion with my hand, showing how it had looked, slightly spiky.

"Oh, I see! I can do that." She squints for a moment before taking a comb from the bottle of blue liquid. "Why did you try to do it yourself?"

"Impatient."

"Right, and you weren't high and got something stuck in it."

What is it with people assuming I'm on drugs? I look from my greenish eyes to hers. My eyes can shift from a yellow-green to muddy brown. They're actually pretty today. "No. I cut it so things wouldn't get stuck in it."

The stylist just nods and bobs to the light rock playing over the speakers. Music. That's something else I've all but forgotten. We had players in some of the vehicles, but there were no radio stations and soon power became too precious to use on something as dumb as a music player. I didn't even miss it.

I leave cash for the stylist and hurry out of the salon. The place creeps me out, too frivolous. That thought stops me in my tracks. I'd always been pretty frivolous before, childish. At this time, the first time, I was busy chatting up my girlfriend Julie and making plans for my birthday. The only care in my world was getting some hot boy to think I was the best thing to walk into his life.

I got that wish. Well, if you could call Heph hot. At this time, the first time, I wouldn't have. He was a bit of a loner with greasy hair and acne. A computer geek. But he also studied martial arts and hunted with his family, which made him the best thing to walk into my life when the meat sacks attacked.

What was I supposed to be doing today? What did I do today, the first time? Work, a summer job at the ice cream shop downtown. Of course, I have no idea what my schedule is any more. Turning onto the right street, I make my way there, hoping I'm not late.

I stop a few times at wolf whistles. When was the last time I heard one of those? The guys at Freetown would check me out, but they were too smart to be obvious like that. Heph would kill them. And if he didn't, I might. They knew that, of course, and kept their thoughts to themselves.

"Hiya, Cassy," Mr. Brown says as I come in. "You're early. You don't start until six."

"Six, right. Would you believe I forgot to write down my schedule for the week?"

He chuckles. "I would. You're on six 'til close Tuesday through Friday. Honestly, I don't know how you can forget something that simple."

"Oh, an apocalypse will do that to you," I mutter quietly. "Thanks, Mr. Brown. I'll see you tonight."

I walk out of the store and straight into a group of girls.

"Cassy! There you are! What did you do to your hair? Never mind. Listen to this. Amy Richardson…"

I immediately tune out the nonsensical information being dropped on me. Do I know an Amy? The girl feeding me the dirt is the same Julie I should be planning my birthday with. Come to think of it, that's probably why she's been looking for me. I barely remember Julie beyond the golden curls cascading around her face. Her hair is almost as nice as mine, almost.

She didn't make it. Looking around the group of girls, I don't recognize a single pretty face. None of them made it. We're all good looking. I wonder if it's the only thing we actually have in common.

"Can you believe it?" Julie finishes.

"I would just die," one of the other girls says. The rest nod in agreement.

"Anyway," Julie continues, "we're obviously not going there. What about you? Have fun in Cali? Something there inspire the new do?" She touches one of my locks and I flinch back a little. It's almost like talking to or being touched by a ghost. She was dead, and now she's alive.

I recover quickly. "Uh, yeah, saw this girl swarmed with guys and liked her hair, y'know?"

Julie nods. "It's nice, but I never thought you'd cut your hair."

I shrug. I can't explain better than I have. "So, party?" I ask, hoping she'll remind me where we're at in the planning.

"Party!" she chimes and the girls around us giggle. "The guest list is currently twenty-five. Your parents won't mind that, right?"

I bite my lip. "I kinda ticked them off on the trip. Let's keep the list as small as possible."

"You did?" Julie asks. Then she shakes her head. "Well, we haven't invited everyone yet, so there's still time to trim. Come on; let's find some accessories for the day." She links her elbow in mine and I start to pull away before forcing myself to relax in her hold. This is the way we used to be, the first time.

I realize that this is the way the world is going be. I stopped it. This is the last time, and for everyone here, it is the first time. Heph has no idea who I am, and Julie will wonder why I'm hanging out with a loner if I track him down. I have to try to remember who I was, to be her again.

It will be hard to be as carefree and clueless as I once was. I have to concentrate to keep up with the inane conversation about colors and gloss and shoes. None of those things have mattered in so long. Well, except shoes. Everyone needs something they can run in. Of course, I'm positive the pair Julie's describing are impossible to walk in, never mind trying to run.

These are my friends. This is my life. Sticking a plastic smile on my face, I put a little bounce in my step. It's the summer of '15, I'm turning eighteen in two weeks, and the world is a wonderful place. I just have to remember that.

I'm not quite able to stop myself from swinging by Heph's house on my way home from work. We've spent every day together for the last eight months. It feels wrong without him. I try to remember if he told me which window belongs to him. I know he's living with his dad, step-mom and step-brothers. Looking at the man watching TV, I immediately recognize Heph's father. Same greasy black hair, same piercing eyes. His dad has wrinkles and shots of grey in his black hair which is receding. He also has a huge nose, which Heph didn't inherit.

He looks my way, startling me, and I trot away, stopping just out of sight of the picture window. There is a light on in one of the upstairs rooms, but I can't see inside. I hear the thundering base line of a heavy piece of rock. My lips curl up. I remember this track. Heph liked to play it on our way out of Freetown — sort of an anthem for entering hell. I wish I could see him.

With a heavy sigh, I head home, trying to be happy to have my mundane, easy life back.

***

On Friday, after several days of longing for his voice, I stop outside Heph's house on my way home from work and call him on my cell.

"Hello?"

"Heph? Is that you?"

"Which one?"

Stupid, cocky... "Jonah. I know it is, so stop being a dick."

"Heh, sorry, just glad to have the phone back. Mom knows how to hit where it hurts."

"Yeah, you've said. You know, you never told me what you were grounded for."

"Who is this?"

Busted. “Um... Cassandra?”

There is a long pause. Too long. *Come on, Heph. Talk to the girl who called you.*

“I don’t know any Cassandras.”

“Yeah, I know you don’t, but I know you and really want you to come to my party.” I fiddle with my purse, opening and closing the metal clasp on the strap. Only a few days, and I’m already happy to have my pretty things back: purses, shoes, skirts. Impractical, but pretty. Old habits, like this one, playing with the clasp, come back without effort. I hope he doesn’t hear the desperation in my request.

“I don’t do parties. Also, I’m still physically grounded. I can only go out with the family.”

“For how long?”

“Who are you?”

“You wouldn’t believe me if I told you.” Suddenly this feels more natural and I lean against the trunk of the elm under his window.

The silence this time is even longer. I check that I’m still connected to the call. Yep. I can almost hear him breathing.

"Heph? It's a girl, asking you on a date. You're supposed to say yes."

"Fine. Friday. I'm grounded until Friday."

"Perfect. My party is on Saturday."

"Will you tell me anyway? Who you are, I mean."

"You really aren't going to believe it." I take a deep breath and then just blurt it out. "I'm from the future, where you and I were very close."

This time the pause isn't quite as long, and I swear I can hear the wheels turning in his brain. "Did we have sex?"

"God, you are such a boy. No, but we probably would have if I hadn't died."

"You died? You're right, I don't believe this."

"It doesn't help that I'm telling it out of order. How about if I prove that I know you? Twenty questions and all that crap. I know your mother lives across town with your sister Abby. That your Mom is actually your stepmom and is a real sadist."

"Heh, she's fair."

“Yeah. Your handle online is KnightRider because that was your Dad’s favorite show growing up.”

“And what was his car named?”

“I don’t know. You didn’t tell me that. You did teach me how to blind an opponent long enough kill him, how to shoot a gun, and how to disarm a security system. I didn’t have much use for that one actually, but hey, good skill.”

“Whoa. I think I’m starting to believe you.”

“I also know you love to sit inside at a desk but you also have a black belt in jujitsu.”

“Okay, and why don’t I live with my mother?”

“Because weepy women give you the creeps.”

“Damn.”

“Please come to my birthday party. I miss you, Heph. I’ve spent the last eight months with you. You’re the only friend from there who is also here. I—” I stop, my voice breaking. If I keep going this way, I’ll freak him out. An idea occurs to me. “You know what else you taught me? How to play that shitty game you’re addicted to. I’ll be online in fifteen minutes, as soon as I get home.

My handle will be Seeress, probably with a bunch of stupid numbers after it. I'll show you what I learned."

"Get home? Where are you?"

"Outside. Under your elm."

The window opens and he sticks out his head. His glasses are halfway down his nose and his acne is terrible. It was when I met him, eight months ago. It amazes me that he didn't scar, but he didn't. He just slowly got more and more handsome. A little muscle here, a little stubble there. Such small changes, but they seem huge when dropped in lump like this. The longer I gaze up, the more I need to look away. He doesn't look like my Heph.

"Holy crap! You're hot! Can we have sex?" He does sound like him. Right down to the single entendre.

"Boys. Not anytime soon." I stick my tongue out at him. "Fifteen minutes. Your ass is mine."

"Sure, sure."

"Heph, will you come to my party?"

"Yeah, I guess so."

"Thanks. I love you."

He doesn't answer, and I don't expect him to. Thinking back to the face I remember and the face I just saw, maybe I don't love this Heph either. I still need him, and anyway, he'll love me more when I take a piece out of him online.

***

Dad's reading the paper at the kitchen table when I get up on Wednesday. "Anything interesting?" I ask around a yawn.

"You tell me," he says passing it over. "I didn't find much. I need to get to work."

Pouring myself a coffee, I pick up the paper and flip through. I've been back in time for a full week and I haven't seen any stories about Dr. Evans, but that might be due the fact that it's an ongoing investigation. From my perspective, no news is the best news. They probably have no idea who did it.

Spoke too soon. There, on page two, is a story about the sudden departure of Dr. Evans and an epidemic spreading through the Manson labs.

Employees in his lab were the first to show symptoms — high fever and delirium.

I don't even read the rest. I run upstairs and grab my phone.

"Heph. It's Cassandra."

"Seeress. What's up? Still reeling from the beating I gave you last night?"

I've met him online four times, and every chat line opens him up to me just a little more. We really are friends now, even though he doesn't quite believe I'm from the future. Didn't stop him asking me for lottery numbers, jackass.

"Har har. No. I need you to get online, get this out to everyone you can under the age of twenty-five. Tell them to head to their nearest sporting goods store and arm themselves. Hole up. Something serious is about to break out."

My mind is racing. We should be able to get the base secure before the internet fails. It will be another day until the virus really takes hold and a week or two after that before major systems — power, sewers, cell service — stop running. It shouldn't take us more than a day or two to claim the base. Of course, we'll have to wait until Friday to take it. No point in getting shot by uninfected soldiers.

"Um, no one's going to listen to me, Cassy." It feels good to hear him use my name. Although we've chatted online, I haven't called him again, and as he just did, he usually called me by my handle, Seeressof2016. No one will listen to him and he won't listen to me. Maybe this is a futile attempt to change the future, but I have to do something.

"They will when you attach footage from the Manson lab in Albuquerque. I'm sure you can find some in the news feeds. If not, grab the picture from the paper. That's going to happen to every adult over the age of twenty-five, and a few under. Damn, we need to get babies. We didn't save nearly enough babies last time." My mind is reeling, trying to remember what we had done and what we wished we had done. How could I have failed?

"Cassy? Are you sure about this?" His mellow voice is shaky. He hasn't started to accept that I came from the future and I don't have time to convince him now. I'm at my computer, trying to remember contact information for as many people from Freetown as I can.

"Yes I'm sure! Heph, get it done. I know you can. I want every teenager who can carry one to be armed with a gun. Once that fever falls, people become animals — flesh-eating monsters. They like uninfected meat best. That's us."

"You're not making sense, Cassy."

Frustrated, I close the window I had opened. It's no use, it's been too long since things like numbers and addresses were important. I'll work through Heph. "I'm coming to your house."

"No! Mom won't let you in."

"Then I'll come through the window. We need to start planning. I'm not losing any more kids than I have to. We'll need all of us if we're going to rebuild."

I disconnect and throw my phone in my bag. I'm just pulling on my shoes when I notice my mother for the first time. She's standing in the doorway, worry line etched between her eyebrows.

"Cassandra? Are you okay?" She comes forward to touch my forehead.

I yank my head back. "I'm fine, Mom. You should probably check yourself. I'm pretty sure you and Dad are going to come down with something in the next twenty-four hours." I pull open the door and hurry out.

"Where are you going?"

"To get reinforcements." She doesn't understand, and she doesn't have to. She isn't the one I'm trying to save.

CHAPTER THREE

"OKAY, I posted the message just like you said." Heph is uneasy, pacing his room. "That's traceable, you know? If a bunch of kids open fire because I posted—"

"Relax, Heph, in two days there isn't going to be anyone to charge you with anything." I'm at his computer reading and writing responses.

He finally sits on his bed. "It's really going to kill them all?"

I take a deep breath. I've never been sure how much of this to share. How much is too much?

"Yes, but no. This virus," I point to the paper on the bed beside him. He sits atop the crumpled blankets, but I've laid it on the sheets for quick reference. "This virus is going to infect everyone. We're already infected. So are our parents, our teachers, police officers, the army—"

"Wait, we're infected?"

I nod. "We're immune, so we don't get sick like they do. We won't turn into meat sacks. We are carriers. The adults don't die, though. The virus can't survive without a living host. A few hours of exposure and it dies. At least that's what Ken told me." I turn back to the monitor and keyboard. "He was a med student, so he should know."

"We get a med student?"

I snicker. "Yep, pre-med but keen enough to work ahead. He was the oldest of us. He died when a section of fence went down." I don't look back at Heph as the tears burn my eyes. I keep typing, half-blind, making a mess of what I'm writing. "If he'd kept a gun on him like we told him, he probably wouldn't have." Ken's red hair and green eyes fill my vision and blur. I blubber a little before wiping my cheeks and sitting up straighter. Grumbling at the typo riddled reply, I start deleting.

Heph's hand closes on my shoulder. It's the first time he's touched me. He's kept his distance since opening the window for me, like touching me might make me real. I can't blame him at all. If I had a magic spell that kept everything I'd witnessed from happening —again— I would. I tried. Frowning, I open a new window.

"What are you doing now?" Heph asks, leaning over my shoulder.

"Why didn't it work? I killed Evans, so who made or distributed the virus?"

Heph doesn't answer and I don't expect he will. We had an all-caps shouting match over the fact that I'd killed someone when I told him. Heph was appalled, but in a strange way, like he was jealous he didn't have something as terrible to confess.

The lab assistants are the first listed victims, so Evans must have released the virus in the lab before he went home that night, and it's been incubating and spreading since then. I've accomplished nothing.

I lean back in the chair and fight tears again. Not despair. I don't have time for that. Remorse? Regret? I had the chance to stop this and I didn't. That is going to haunt me.

"Cassy?"

I open my eyes to see Heph's face upside down over mine. His nose is bigger than I remember. Still not as big as his Dad's, or maybe it's just because I've never looked straight up his nostrils before.

"We're going to be okay, right?" he asks, though I can tell he's actually reassuring me.

I smile, small and wry, sitting up enough to kiss the tip of his nose. "Yep. We're going to be fine. We're going to be better this time; if people listen to me anyway."

"Who's not going to listen to you? You just told them to get guns. What kid doesn't want to handle a gun?"

I laugh and have to cover my mouth to muffle it. There's enough music in this room and the next that I haven't worried about anyone hearing me speak, but this case of the giggles could get loud.

"Actually, there are a few, but you're right. Most are flocking to do our bidding." I laugh again. "I wonder how long until they have to fight."

"You don't know?"

I shake my head. "I have a general idea. Our parents are going to succumb soon, but when exactly each group of adults falls is a little random. By tomorrow there will be more meat sacks that doctors will try to save, until they fall themselves. Actually, the hospitals go pretty fast. Do you know if anyone followed my lead on the babies?" I start clicking back through pages of posts and replies.

"Yeah. One did. What was her name?" Heph's hand replaces mine on the mouse. I watch his long fingers curl over the grey plastic. The parting between his thumb and forefinger reminds me of how he holds a blade; the clicking reminds me how he shoots a gun. It's only been a little over a week since I came back here, a week without him, but I've missed him so much. My fingers stretch toward his.

"Annie1129."

"Jenny?" I ask, pulling my hand away quickly. Smiling broadly, I look at the post from Jennifer Anne. Annie online, Jenny in real life. In her case, the numbers aren't garbage but her birthday, November 29th.

I didn't have many friends in Freetown. Everyone knew everyone else, but we were all cagey as well. You didn't know when someone might not come back from a raid or a section of fencing would go down. We didn't tend to get close with one another. Jenny was an exception. She didn't pull away from anyone, trying to be there for everyone. She was the mother of Freetown, figuratively and literally. I'd been there when she gave birth.

"You know her too?"

Smiling, I remember Jenny. Her blond hair is straight and fine, blowing in the slightest breeze and annoying with static in the winter. She's skinny at first and then gets larger and larger until I'm sure her belly isn't actually a part of her anymore. In a way it isn't; it's Patience. Jenny, her blue eyes full of love and compassion. It's no surprise she doesn't want to touch a gun.

"Yes, and I know why she'd be keen to gather babies. What I don't know is how she plans to keep the meat sacks off her. She isn't a fighter. She hates violence."

"That'll change though, right?"

I shake my head. "Not for her. As soon as we secure Freetown, she spends all her time there, making a garden, decorating, teaching and entertaining the littlest ones. She leaves the perimeter and all fighting to the rest of us."

"Great. How nice of her."

"You don't understand. She's really good at that, nurturing, and almost no one else will be. She knows how to cook, like, really well, not just mac and cheese. There are a lot of younger kids that we can save, but if we can't look after them... She's really good with kids, which is good, because she's going to be a mom before long."

"Okay, you've lost me again. Forget them," Heph says, putting his hand between me and the monitor. I suppress a sigh and turn to face him. "You said we're not going to a sporting goods store."

I chuckle. "No, your dad has more than enough guns here."

He nods reluctantly. "Yeah, I guess so. He is a hunter after all."

"I know, that's how you know how to shoot and were able to teach me." I sigh happily. "I'm so glad I won't have to learn that over again."

"So, we aren't stocking arms and ammo. What are we doing?"

"Liberating Freetown."

"Okay. Where is Freetown."

I grin widely. "Want to guess?"

"Here? Gallup?"

I snort. "Yeah, right. First, have you seen how far these replies are coming from? We need somewhere more central. We need somewhere armed but that's easy to close off. Big enough to house a few thousand of us."

"An army base."

I nod. "Fort Carson, actually. At least, that worked last time."

"Okay, so Freetown is Fort Carson and you want to liberate it?!" Heph seizes both my shoulders roughly. "You're talking about going up against trained soldiers!"

"Settle down!" My voice is raspy as I try to keep it lower than his. "They won't be soldiers anymore, or at least, most of them won't. If any were immune last time, they fell to the meat sacks. I'm not suggesting going in now, only half of them will even be sick, but in two days, everyone who is infected will be a mindless walking husk. Anyone who isn't will be trying to stay alive. People usually appreciate help when that happens."

Heph huffs. "I don't know, Cassy. This sounds crazy. How did you do it last time?"

I shudder a little at the memory. "Very messily. We lost a lot of people on our way to somewhere we could defend. In fact, you and I were still holed up here when word came that Carson was safe."

"Then you weren't part of taking the base last time? Are you sure you want to try? Who did take it?"

I knew he was going to ask that. "A cadet troop."

He throws his hands in the air. "And you really think the pair of us can do what a cadet troop did? Those guys are trained too, Cass."

I don't meet his eye for a minute. "I'm just making a plan—"

"I don't think you quite realize what you're asking of me, of everyone. I'm amazed anyone is listening to us. We sound like a pair of crazy teenagers. 'The end of the world is coming, fear for your lives.' There's a reason that number isn't higher." He points to the stats bar on our webpage. "You need to go slow, Cassy. Scaring people isn't the way to start."

I feel tears of frustration forming and hate them. "I just want to stop this. I don't want . . ."

"Oh, shit. Don't cry. Damn it. Please, Cassy, don't cry."

I laugh a little. "You never cry. Even when . . ." I choke for a minute, remembering him telling me how he'd shot his parents to escape the house. That won't be happening this time. I can fix some things. I wipe my cheeks roughly. "Sorry. You're right. Slow. That's good. Gathering is important. We can fight them off better together. We don't need to aim for the base now."

Heph's smile is tight, unwilling to respond to weeping women. "You are one weird girl, Cassy. I still don't quite believe you, but at the same time, I can't not believe you."

I sniffle and wipe at my nose. "I'm glad you can't. I need someone in all of this." I reach out and grab his shoulders, hugging him, and landing heavily in his lap.

"Uh. Yeah. I'm here for you." His hands move over my back, never quite stopping in any one place. He's stiff in my arms, stiffer than I remember. Backing up, I see why. He has a look of terror on his face that I've only seen a few times before. I chuckle and slide from his lap to the bed beside him. I lean my head into his.

"You're the best friend ever, Heph. I'm sorry I'm dumping on you like this. I know you hate whiny people dropping things for someone else to pick up."

"Whoa. Hold on there. You aren't doing that."

My hand moves toward his, tracing his long slender fingers, fitting mine between them. "Right. Well, thanks for understanding, for not being completely creeped out. I really do need you."

"I can tell. You need more than just me. Was there anyone else?"

I close my eyes for a moment, remembering. "Not in town. By the time we made it out, there were only about twenty of us. I plan to make that more. If I have to arm my birthday party and storm out of it, I will do it."

Heph gets a confused look on his face that makes me start laughing again. "My parents' fevers broke the day of my party, last go around, and they started attacking my guests. We all ran screaming in different directions and my dad took out three girls quickly. Mom wasn't far behind. I made it out of the yard. None of the others did. Well, I assume they didn't. I never saw them again; my silly, shallow, normal friends. Not like you. Survivor friends, they're different." I continue to hold his hand in my lap, squeezing now and again.

"I'll take your word on that. I've never had one before. I've never had a girlfriend. Is that what we were? I know I asked before, but I'm curious now. Did we?" He brushes my bangs back from my eyes and I have to close them against all the memories I have, all the days and nights we shared as comrades, as two warm bodies huddled against the cold, as mentor and teacher, as much more than friends.

I feel his lips on mine and run with the memories, remembering the last time he kissed me, the last time I wrapped myself around him. I want to feel more of him, all of him. He feels a little different, more stiff and less rigid at the same time. Muscles that were hard are not and tension is replacing their strength.

It takes effort but I rein myself in, breaking the kiss. I'm lying atop him on his bed. I really shouldn't have let things get this far. He's bright red, breathing hard, and obviously wishing I hadn't stopped.

"I'm sorry, Heph. It's you, but it isn't, y'know?"

He shakes his head, still not quite able to speak. I notice his shirt is pulled up and reach out to fix it. His hand brushes at it first, yanking the fabric down. He's embarrassed, probably feeling a little hurt.

"Soon, maybe?" I offer. I certainly want to do that, and more, but I want him to know me, not be washed away in my memories. Knowing him, he'd be just as happy either way.

I shake my head a little at the thought. "No?" he asks. "Not again?"

Snickering, I answer. "Not that. It's nothing. Listen, I think we've done enough for tonight. I can keep a tab on this from my place now. Don't worry about any authorities tracing you, worry about your parents. I don't want any more crap coming down on you."

"Good point. I don't want anything more heaped on this sentence." He deflates a little at the reminder that he is still confined to the house.

"What did you do to get grounded anyway?"

"Nothing. You should go. Mom'll probably come check on me sometime tonight."

A little upset at being evaded again, I frown as I make my way out the window. "I'll call you tomorrow after my shift. Call me if anything big comes up before then?"

"Wouldn't you know about it first? I mean, I thought you came from the future."

He does believe me. Still, I'm not perfect. "Things have changed. I've started people moving. I don't know what else might change."

"Oh, right. And, uh, if you need more—" He moves toward me, arms open for a hug.

"No!" I shout, throwing up a hand and nearly falling over the sill. "No more of that until you know me like I know you." Without any other parting words, I fall from the window to catch a thick branch of the elm and then drop to the ground.

***

I push through two more days. My friends of this time don't believe me, and I've alienated all of them with my constant warnings. Julie isn't talking to me and has officially declared my party, "the worst place to be in 2015." I laugh a little when I hear that. It's rather true. My parents made a real mess of my party the first time. Neither I nor my friends will be here on Saturday.

I'm gaining a little traction online. As Albuquerque starts to fall apart, people are taking the hint that maybe this virus is actually a bad thing. Medical people are still trying to analyze it, which means they're succumbing. Manson closed shop and their stock plummeted to nothing after word got out that their accounting department was eaten by their research staff. That much, at least, is the same as the first time. Also the same as the first time, no one associates the two. No one seems to put together the failed experiment, the murdered doctor, and the flesh-eating frenzy the Manson staff and many other random people are suffering from.

Some adults are following me online. They are desperate for some assurance that they can escape it. There's little I can do for them. I tell them to isolate themselves. If they have a relative on a farm, go there and don't let anyone come near the house. It's the best I have for them.

There is also the hate contingent. They constantly flame me. Adults call me an anarchist. Anarchists call me crazy. Religious people claim I don't have enough faith. Atheists claim I don't have scientific evidence. Mostly, they call me a liar. I keep my skin thick and push on. I can only help those who listen. All I can do is get the word out.

The majority of people, they don't have a clue what's going on. The news is claiming there's a new form of flu, "rabbit flu" or something ridiculous like that. They're stocking up on cold remedies and buying masks, as though that might protect them. For some it will, for a little while, but this thing is too strong. They'll slip some time, and that's all the virus needs.

I know that my experience is only good for saving me and those immediately around me. It's hard to accept, and I spend hours a day screaming at the idiots on my monitor who could save themselves if they'd only listen.

I stop at Heph's both nights after work.

"You know you're going to have to sneak out of here, right?"

"What do you mean?" he asks, looking up from the game he's been playing since I arrived.

"I mean, your parents are going to get sick and you're going to have to leave them."

His character dies suddenly as he's distracted by what I've said. "Mom's got a fever."

"See?" I tell him. "Your Dad won't be far behind. You and your brothers need to go."

Heph shakes his head. "No. I can't leave them. Also, Connor has a fever, too." That's his oldest step-brother. "I had to make supper for them tonight. They'll need me tomorrow."

I close my eyes and fight frustration. "Heph, do you believe me or not?"

"I believe you."

"Then understand that you can't help them. If you stay, they'll attack you and you'll have to kill them."

He chuckles. "Nah, they don't have that virus. They just have this flu."

I grab his shoulders and turn him to look at me. "It's the same virus. They're going to turn into meat sacks. The only thought in their head will be to find fresh meat, and you'll look mighty tasty. Now get the key to the gun locker, arm us up, and let's go."

"What about your parents? Are they sick? Aren't you worried about them?" He looks at me like maybe he doesn't want to know me. I can't really blame him.

I sigh and say, "My parents died eight months ago. I thought I got them back, but I was wrong. I've already mourned my parents, Heph. Don't get killed mourning yours." I stand up and move to the window, but his hand closes on my arm.

"Wait, Cassy. I do believe you. I just didn't think. They're my family."

Turning back, I see the pain on his face. It's very familiar. "I know where we can find a new family. We can't save this one." I shake my head a little and then wrap my arms around his waist, crushing him to me in a hug. Tears choke my voice. "Knowing won't save a single one of them. I tried, Heph. I really tried. I thought if I killed Evans, this would all go away; we'd all be safe, but I couldn't save a single person."

"Don't cry, Cassy." His voice is full of irritation and it stems the flow quickly. He really can't stand weepers or complainers. "You saved a few more people."

He's right. I've done what I could with the crap I had. "Who knows, maybe I'll get another chance to do this again. I can do better next time."

His mouth twists in a grimace. "Wouldn't that mean you'd have to die again?"

I shrug. “I guess so. I don’t have any intentions of dying soon, but let’s face it, our future isn’t exactly safe.”

“I’ll steal the guns tonight, okay?” he puts his forehead to mine and I cringe a little at the oily feel of his skin. That gets better in the next months. “Then I’ll meet you outside somewhere.”

I nod, my head rubbing against his, increasing the uncomfortable feeling. “I’ll be in the beige Ford Taurus at the end of the block.”

His nose wrinkles. “A beige Taurus?”

I step back and chuckle. “Trust me, in a few months, you are going to love that car.”

Jumping from the window, I head home. Mom and Dad don’t even question why I’m late coming home anymore. I’ve given them lies that they don’t accept and the truth, which they accept even less. I do come home each night, usually before midnight, always before two, so they don’t have any big complaints. Tonight no one questions me. Dad is passed out on the couch with a cloth on his head.

“Denver, fetch boy. Fetch.” He’s calling to our dog that was hit by a car when I was ten. My eyes fill with tears, knowing what’s coming next. I can’t help him or Mom. I see her lying in the tub, shivering.

“So cold,” she murmurs. “Why can’t I get warm?” In fact, the water is steaming slightly and I know without getting closer that she’s even warmer than it is. Her brain is slowly being cooked. It’s horrible. Is it better to let them live? Let them become a walking nightmare? Or should I kill my parents as Heph did the first time?

Standing in the bathroom doorway for another moment, eyes locked on my naked shivering mother, I realize I can’t kill them.

In my room, I pull out a bag filling it with anything practical I can find. Warm clothes go in first. I don’t have many of those, and we’ll be able to loot more, but I don’t want to be caught without. Next are my toiletries; same reason. I grab some of the camping gear, the Coleman gas stove, the enamelware. I lug the first load out the car.

It must have taken a while because my Mom is out of the tub and standing in the entry way, hair dripping. “Where do you think you’re going, young lady?”

“Camping, with Julie,” I lie easily.

“Oh, well make sure you take Mr. Tickle with you,” she says turning back into the house. “Gosh, I’m hungry.” Not sure who Mr. Tickle is, and not really caring, I run back into the house, slipping past Mom to get the sleeping bags and tent. Losing her balance, she falls to the floor, not getting up. She doesn’t complain, another sign she’s losing to the bug inside her.

I drive to Heph’s and lean back in the seat to wait. My eyes are heavy, so I lock the doors before closing them and napping behind the wheel. It’s not comfortable, but a couple weeks haven’t gotten me out of the habit of catching a nap when I can.

I wake to a scratching and open my eyes in blinks. “Heph?” I ask.

I scream at the face in my window. Bloody gashes cover one side of it and the chin and shirt are also covered in blood. Most importantly, the eyes are pale with huge empty pupils. Meat sack. A few deep breaths get me over my fright and I start the engine, throwing the car in reverse. The mindless creature falls as the support is pulled away from under him. I put it in drive and park atop him, continuing to wait for Heph. I won't leave without him.

The handle snaps as he tries to get in. I unlock the door quickly.

"Oh my God, Cassy," he says as he opens it. "There's a guy under your front tire, trying to pull himself out."

"Yeah, he'll be able to get up soon." There's some clattering as he sets the butts of two rifles on the floor of the car.

"But, he's still trying."

"The virus doesn't let them feel pain, they don't die quickly."

"My brother woke up."

I suck in a breath and look away from him.

“He tried to bite me, Cassy. I barely got away from him. They’re stronger, aren’t they?” From the corner of my eye, I watch him work his shoulder. I decide to change the topic.

“What did you bring me?” I ask, smiling sweetly.

He chuckles in a familiar way. “For you, Seeress, I have a Winchester.” He passes it over like a bouquet of flowers, the other rifle leans on the door.

“How thoughtful of you,” I say, batting my lashes and holding hand to heart before accepting the gun. It’s light, around seven pounds, making it easy to handle. I set it down on the back seat atop my suitcase.

“Should I have brought more than guns?” he asks, looking at the bag and putting his gun down as well.

“Are you willing to go back in there to get it?” I ask, cocking my head toward his house down the block.

"No," he agrees in a heartbeat. "Let's go." After I've pulled away, he asks, "Where are we going?"

I look at him for a moment before turning back to the relatively deserted road. I notice one or two cars in the ditch. Likely the drivers became too sick.

"You're not serious. You, me and, two guns are going to take an army base?"

"Don't you check your messages?" I ask, looking to the stars. "I have a group of five waiting for us in Fort Carson. They're coming down from Denver. We aren't doing this alone."

"Cassy, I don't know if I can shoot a person."

I nod. "I had that problem at first. Look in their eyes. You can see it there. They aren't human anymore. They're feral, vacant. You don't mind putting them out of their misery or preventing your own after looking into their eyes."

He gulps. "I don't know if I want you for a girlfriend."

I laugh. “Well, that can still be changed. Just be glad you don’t have to be cornered with me while I’m still learning how to shoot.”

“We had some close calls, did we?”

“More than a few. I was so useless at first. I mean, I could run, but that was about it. You taught me how to fight. You didn’t have any trouble killing a meat sack when I found you.”

“Tell me about it? Seeing as we have a bit of a drive ahead of us.”

I haven’t shared much about the past, or the future. It’s gotten a little muddied in my head. Of course, those specific incidents aren’t likely to happen again. That makes me feel a little bit better about sharing specifics.

“I was running scared. My entire party had been wiped out by my parents, and I had no idea where to go. Dawn came and I was still stumbling, avoiding the people spilling into the street, the people eating each other. Finally, I came to the cop shop.”

“No way! You went to the cops?”

"I thought they could help me. Of course, the place was empty. The few people on night shift must have been infected. I slept in a cell downstairs, locked myself in."

"Why'd you do that?"

"So they couldn't get me."

"Weren't you afraid you couldn't get out?"

"At that point, I was just afraid of being eaten. I wasn't thinking past getting some rest. That's where you found me."

"I found you?"

I nod, smiling. "That's right. You had a posse by then, but you weren't able to get your Dad's locker key. You came looking for guns and found me."

"I had a posse? Who was in it?"

I shake my head. "I don't remember. They were sloppy and most got picked off. There wasn't anywhere safe in Gallup. Some sacks could remember how to open doors, some were never able to leave their houses. So you never knew, walking into a building, if there was a group waiting inside, or if a group would follow you in. We gathered up a few people. Then the fire broke out and the few of us fled together."

"Where'd we go?"

"Albuquerque."

Heph snorts. "Because a bigger city with more monsters will be safe."

I chuckle, too. "Something like that. You'd heard there was a group there, holding out in one of their police stations. We didn't realize then that we were hiding where the whole thing began."

"I thought Manson's lab was—"

I laugh at the irony, interrupting him. "It was. The station was at the end of the block. We must have hidden two weeks before we heard that Fort Carson had become Freetown. So, we all loaded up in one of the Police vans and drove north."

"Two weeks," Heph muses, looking in the backseat. "What did we live on?"

"That's how we lost some people. We'd loot grocers."

Heph nods. "No one to stop you."

"Everyone to stop us, but not from looting, from breathing."

Heph shudders beside me. "You're sure taking Carson now is a good idea? I mean, weeks. Certainly, some of these things die off after a few weeks."

I snort. "They don't die off, Heph. They eat each other when there isn't anything better, but they don't just die. So yeah, there were probably less the first time. They'll still be meat sacks, possibly with a few young trainees who aren't infected and glad for the help."

"Meat sack. Is there a reason we don't call them zombies?"

I shrug. There isn't really, it just sounded unreal that way, fictitious. Of course, meat sack isn't a lot better; it was just what caught on.

"So, I was pretty badass?" Heph asks, grinning.

"You are pretty badass," I tell him, grinning as well. "I've never seen anyone take the head off one of those things like you. Blade especially. I was never as good at that, though you said I was one of your best students."

He sighs and sinks down into the seat with a yawn.

"Go on and sleep. I had a nap before you came out. I'll wake you when I need you to drive."

He nods and turns his head away from me. There's something comforting about him sleeping with me. In the past, it was a sign that he trusted me to watch his back, that he trusted me enough to leave his life in my hands. It might not mean quite that much now, but it brings the memory back. After several minutes, I rest my hand on his neck and feel his pulse and breathing under my fingers. I run my nails lightly through his hair. I have Heph; I can do this. Again.

CHAPTER FOUR

FORT CARSON is looking better than I expect. I've forgotten how small the town is. The infection will take longer to reach here. Heph is going to be horrible when he hears. "I told you so," is one of his favorite phrases. In the meantime, I need to find Brian and the others.

Only a few vehicles are moving on the streets, but it's hard to tell if that's because it's early in the morning or people are in bed, infected. I keep my eye out for a blue van, Brian and his group should be in it. I see a lot of pickup trucks including some nice old ones. We'll have to make sure we hold on to some of those.

Heph snorts and starts beside me. "Huh? Geez, Cass," he complains while stretching and rubbing his eyes. "You should have woken me to drive."

I shrug. "I'm still good. Help me find a blue van. We have to stop them before they hit the base on their own. They were pretty eager, crazy anarchists." The last is muttered.

"Why not let them do it? You want a piece of the action that bad?"

I fight a groan. "No. We're too early. There aren't any meat sacks in the street, which means there probably aren't many on the base. We're going to have to spend a few days in town."

His smirk is familiar and infuriating.

"Well, it must be relatively safe here. Where should we go?"

"It's not safe anywhere, Heph." I can't quite believe how different this Heph is from the one I knew. The more I get to know him, in his less defensive form, the more I miss my Heph. He wouldn't be looking for somewhere to hang out.

He'd be searching for resources while they are available, finding a place we could hold together. The only thing this Heph has in common with mine would be the fact that neither has much desire to find Brian and his group. My Heph would say that, if they were stupid enough to charge the base on their own, they deserved what they got. Did I mention his favorite phrase is "I told you so?"

"Okay, so let's make somewhere safe." He reaches into the backseat for his rifle.

I grab his hand. "I'm sorry. I forget that you don't know what I do, that you haven't seen this happen before. We can't shoot anyone. They aren't meat sacks yet."

"Right," he grumbles, sitting back. "So, what do you want me to do, Cassy? I'm not some hero who is going to jump in and save the world. That's your department."

I glare at him from the corner of my eye. His clothing is familiar, dark cargo pants and t-shirt. His lean arms are crossed over his chest, showing the broadness there. He isn't beefy, he's wiry. He was a hero.

"I'm not a hero either. I'm just the girl who has seen this before, and saving people became your department. You were quick to volunteer for rescue missions."

He slouches and doesn't answer me. I figure that means I need to keep talking.

"You can help me look for Brian. You can fill the tank at the gas station. You can stop moping." I hear the irritation creeping into my voice too late.

Heph sits up. "Well, excuse me. I'm sorry I wasn't able to accept your story quickly enough. I'm sorry I'm not more helpful to you. Maybe I should just take my guns and-"

"Wait," I interrupt. "Heph, it's been a long day, a long night. I probably just need some sleep. Why don't you drive for a while? See if you can find a blue van with six guys, our age. They're coming from the north, so try that side of town."

I open my door to trade seats, but Heph doesn't follow my example. I circle around and lean in the lowered window. He's pouting. I try to recall ever seeing that before and can't. Smiling a little at the innocent expression, so different from the arrogance, the hardness that I see normally, I brush his lips with mine.

He sighs and reaches for the door handle, finally uncrossing his arms.

"Thank you, Heph." I lean back the seat and close my eyes. I don't know if sleeping in his presence will mean the same to him, but I fake it anyway. He needs to know I trust him. Unfortunately, I don't trust him. This Heph isn't as decisive, hasn't fought his way out of a corner, hasn't woken at the last moment to see blood stained jaws descending toward his neck. My eyes are closed, but I'm not asleep.

He fills at a gas station where someone isn't home sick. I'm almost surprised there are any of those. I would have just gone inside, flipped the switch and filled at a deserted station, but his way works. As long as he still has some way to pay. I didn't even bring cash. It becomes useless so quickly. We're too busy doing all the things necessary to keep our new home running, together, that we don't need a sign of individual wealth. Maybe, after a few more months, we would have started using it symbolically in barter exchanges, but we were so dependent on each other, I'm not sure we would have.

I crack an eye open the second time he turns off the ignition. I can't see much beyond the glare of the summer sun. Once my eyes adjust, I see part of a blue van. I have to fight the urge to jump up and out of the car. He can do this; it's better to let him do this.

A shadow passes over me and there is a knock at the window. I blink blearily and open the door slowly.

"Cassy? You want to meet Brian?"

I groan as I stretch dramatically. Heph smiles, but that's as likely for my breasts as my display of trust. "Yes. Hi Brian, thanks for coming."

"Thanks for the heads up. My parents went down yesterday, fever and crazy talk, just like you said. Glad we have you on our side."

I smile and shake his hand, using it to pull myself out of the car. "Well, I'm afraid this show is on hold for the moment."

"Yeah, that's what Heph was saying. Not enough infection here yet? How does that work? How does it spread?"

I grimace a little. I was never much good at biology but I already know more than I ever wanted about this virus. "It's airborne but needs a host. So until someone sick came here, or another carrier like us, the town wouldn't be infected. Of course, everyone is travelling somewhere, people arriving and leaving, so it spreads fast. It's also slow to incubate, so people will spread it before they know they're sick. It must have taken a little longer for someone to bring it here. It's here, though. I can tell."

"You can?" Brian asks.

"Where are all the people?" I hold my arms out. "Home, sick. Let's use the time to round up some locals and get back online. We won't have power and cell service for much longer, unless something changes."

I lead the boys away, the only girl in the group. It doesn't bother me. I was surrounded by guys a lot the first time. They tend to be better fighters than the girls and able to get out. The girls we had, like me, were almost all runners.

Our pack descends on the mall. The guys crack jokes about me needing to shop, but I ignore them. They shut up when half the shops are closed but twenty or thirty kids mill the halls. The few people working are in their early twenties at the oldest. I find the info booth, which isn't staffed and hop the counter.

"What are you doing?" Heph asks.

I ignore him and look around the desk. Finally, I pick up the old fashioned hand set phone and push one of the red buttons. "Attention, residents of Fort Carson."

"Holy crap, did she just—?"

"She did," Heph answers the astonished boy.

I don't pause. "Your town has been infected. Most of the adults are at home with a fever. Some have started seeing things that aren't there. This is the first stage. Soon the fever will peak and they will crave meat—raw, living meat. Us. If you don't want to be caught in the open when that happens, come to the Information Booth."

Several people gather as soon as I finish, wondering who I am and what I'm doing. Before jumping the counter again, I send one more message, "And don't worry about your shops. Everywhere is infected. Head office isn't coming for anyone. Close up and come on over."

"Who are you?" Someone asks as I heft myself onto the counter. Heph takes my hand and Brian's group make a small circle around me as I jump down.

"What do you mean, living meat?"

"How do you know?"

"What should we do?"

I frown. The group is larger than I expected. I was hoping to save more people, but for the first time I worry about over-capacity.

"Stay calm. I didn't steal or break anything. I've seen this virus before. My parents turned into flesh-eating zombies, and I had to run or be killed. Most of my friends were killed." True, all of that happened the first time, not this time, but they didn't need to know that part.

"How do you know that's what our parents have?"

"Because it's spreading. Because it looks just like I described." I have to convince them. I can't have a group this large against me. "When was the last time your parents were delirious? This isn't a normal sickness. They aren't going to get better."

"Why aren't we sick?" a girl asks.

"Because we're immune. We carry the virus but it doesn't affect us. It doesn't affect most people under twenty."

"What should we do?"

"Okay, right now the adults are still conscious, mostly. We don't want to hurt them, but we need to go somewhere that we'll be safe. We should take the base."

"Fight soldiers?"

"You can't be serious."

"Are you crazy?"

"How do you know all this?"

I fight against frustration with the mob. "Look, the soldiers are sick just like everyone else. We go in and push them all out. Just push. If they're running that fever and seeing things, it shouldn't be hard to shove them out."

"And if they're not?"

"We take them in. They're probably younger and won't get sick. Then we lock the doors behind the others and hunker down."

"Doesn't sound like much of a plan. Where are we going to get food? How are we going to live in there?"

"There is a mess and barracks. The food won't run out soon, and we can get more from here," I explain.

"How do you know all this?" It's the same boy asking every time. He has flaming red hair and stands a little taller than most of the crowd.

"I know because I've seen it happen. I've done this once before and built Freetown on Fort Carson. I was given the chance to come back and warn everyone." I still think I'd had the chance to stop the whole thing. Mentioning that, however, is a good way to get everyone screaming for my head.

"She is crazy," I hear someone whisper.

"I think my 'rents aren't the only ones seeing things."

"There is no way I'm living on the base."

I close my eyes and wait for another shouted question, but none come.

"Okay, guys, let's get out of here." I look to my guard and follow them out of the mall. I take the lead from there and follow the signs to the local library. "Internet anyone?" I say with a smile.

The library is locked up, probably all the librarians are sick, but a rock to the window lets me enter and open the door for everyone.

“You’re really destructive, you know that?” Heph comments as his boots crunch on broken glass.

“Yeah? You kinda get used to it when everything is broken and dirty all the time. Come on.” I find the lights and we claim a couple of the desks. Brian and his group come close but look lost. “Go on,” I say pointing at the next desk down. “Send a message to everyone you know to make their way to Fort Carson, Freetown. We should have the base long before they get here. If they don’t believe you now, they will soon. Or they might be dead.” I shrug and continue typing, replying to a message from Jennifer Anne. She’s hunkering down in a local day care. With a group of girls, she’s going to hit several more and bring whoever they find. I hope a few of the day care workers are young enough to come along. I sense there are going to be a lot more babies to sit this time.

We crash in the library that night, pooling cash to order pizzas. It’s not really a surprise to find people at the door when we go to pay.

Outside the library, I encounter a large group of teens, some younger kids as well, even a few toddlers. One of these runs forward and grabs onto my legs.

"Mom tried to bite me!" the little girl wails.

I bend down and pick her up. She's probably five, and shaking with tears and fear. "Shhh, sweetie. I know it's scary. We're going to take you somewhere safe, okay? None of the bad monsters are going to bite you." I look to the crowd, with the little girl burying her face in my shoulder. "I take it all of you have had something similar happen?"

There are nods all around and I see a few bloody hands. Some probably had to fight their way out.

"Then it's time. Let's make Freetown." Carrying the girl with me, I take her into the library for one last night before hell breaks loose.

***

It's a sign of the infection's spread that there is only one soldier at the gate. He looks about ready to fall over. His eyes are blurred and unable to focus properly. Or rather, they're focusing on something none of us can see. I lift my rifle, expecting him to move or raise his weapon, but he does neither.

"Wait, Cassy," Heph puts a hand on the top of my gun. I look from him to the group of children and teens behind me.

Putting the butt of the rifle to my foot, I turn to face them. "You might as well learn the signs of infection now. You've seen them in your parents and teachers. They're sweaty with fever; their eyes go wide and see things that aren't there, then they pass out."

There is a soft thud behind me and I turn to see the soldier crumpled on the ground. Nice example.

"As soon as you see those symptoms, it's too late. They're only minutes or hours from becoming a monster. It's faster, and easier, to kill them now." I lift the rifle again and point it to the soldier's head. The bullet passes through his brain to the ground with a small red spray to show for it. The recoil against my shoulder is familiar. I sigh a little, knowing I'm doing my part; I'm making us all safer. I lower the rifle, looping the strap over my head and turn again.

"There will be many soldiers in there that are sick. There will be some that have already changed. I hope there are a few who are neither. We kill all the rest. I won't say it's a mercy. I don't know what living like one of them is like. But it is us versus them. They will kill us if we don't kill them first."

"Do you have any more guns?" someone in the crowd asks.

"No, but I'm pretty sure we can find some in there." I cock my head to the gate. "Anyone under sixteen or who doesn't want to be a part of this, wait just inside the gate. Close it. You'll be safer inside."

I stride through the gate, stepping over the body of the soldier. I don't look at him; he's just another meat sack. There is a light clatter as someone grabs his gun.

Heph is quick to join me at my side. "I didn't know you were an inspirational speaker," he says with mild sarcasm. "Those who aren't drooling at the thought of firing a gun are scared shitless."

"They should be," I tell him, softening finally. "This world sucks. I hate that I didn't stop it. The least I can do is try to make it better sooner. Look out." I tell him, ducking back around the corner.

The man in army fatigues has gone completely feral. He has blood on his face and hands and he snarls when he sees us around the corner. Heph, in a move I recognize, swings his rifle like sword blade, clipping the man over the ear and sending him to the ground. The soldier doesn't stay down, of course. In seconds, he's pushing himself up again, but a second is all Heph needs to shoot him.

He's shaking a little, and I put a hand on his shoulder. "All right? Last time you'd killed many before I met you. I remember killing my first." He'd been with me, coaching me, and rubbed my back when I vomited. Heph doesn't vomit. He shakes a little longer and then straightens.

"He really was just an animal." After another moment, he adds, "I can shoot animals."

I smile grimly. It's the only way any of us can really accept what we do.

"He came from that direction." I point. "So let's go that way." I point down another corridor.

There are grunts of agreement from behind me. Again, I'm one of the only girls in a sea of boys. I can count four others, but that's it. Well, the fewer of us who have to learn to do this, the better.

We make our way down several corridors, all looking much like the one before. We run into several packs of sick soldiers, most feral, and put them all down quickly. In one room, we kill five and find their guns nearby, arming more of us.

Eventually we make our way to the armory. I dodge back around a corner as a gun fires. Thankfully I'm in the lead, not one of the boys that probably wouldn't have been as quick to react.

"Wait! We're not sick. We're not animals," I call around the corner. "We're here to help."

“Identify yourself.”

Slinging the rifle on my back, I motion the others to lower their guns. Then I step out with my hands up.

“I’m Cassandra. I’m here to help you stop the others.”

“What unit?” the soldier with brush cut mousy hair asks, rifle still trained on me.

“I’m not—” I’m interrupted by a snarl as a meat sack comes from another direction. He runs right at me, not inhumanly fast, but at a dead sprint. I sidestep and throw out hip and hand, whirling him as well as myself in a circle, with me coming down on top. The heel of my hand smashes his nose into his face, knocking him out for the moment it takes Heph to bring his gun back up and shoot.

“I didn’t give you permission to fire,” the skinny soldier guarding the door shouts.

“And I didn’t give you permission to watch her be eaten,” he shouts back. “We’re civilians, all of us.” He pauses for a moment before doing what I least expect. “Think about it. What’s happening here is happening everywhere. There isn't going to be a US Army left in a few days." I know it's merely what I've been telling him, trying to prepare him for, but I feel pride when he steps forward and says it himself.

The soldier reels for just a moment, considering that. Finally, slowly, he lowers his rifle and Heph does the same.

"If you're civilian, why are you here?"

I answer this time, rising and dabbing at blood on my shoulder. "Because it's a safe place. We can defend this against all the meat sacks that come."

"Meat sack? What are you talking about?" the soldier asks.

I point to the corpse on the floor. "That. Brainless towers of flesh, walking around looking for more flesh to eat; a sack of meat running on his last pair of neurons, so few, in fact, that they don't stop for pain. They don't die short of a kill shot. We face a whole country of those, but the people who don't get sick, the immune and young need somewhere safe to live. Will you deny us this place?"

"You're here for guns," he accuses.

"Yes," I answer quickly. "And grenades if you have them. We want to eradicate the base as soon as possible and let the others know where to come."

"Why this base?"

I shrug. "It's the one we chose the first time, but I don't know why. It was established before I got here. It's central. It's large. Why not this base?"

He mouths "first time" and I kick myself for running on at the mouth. However, he eventually shrugs and says, "Well, seeing as you shot the CO, I guess I'll have to find the next in command. I'm not arming you. I'm not letting anyone through this door."

There's a knock from inside, then a pounding. "Open it!"

When the door swings open, a stocky young soldier falls to the ground and six meat sacks charge out. I still haven't pulled my rifle up, but

Heph and the boys with me are ready. All six go down in a heartbeat. I can't help but smirk as mister cocky soldier is stuck watching.

"Well, I guess that's it then. The only other person left is Micky, but I doubt he let you in."

I nod, remembering the delirious soldier at the gate. Then I kneel next to the fallen soldier, the stocky one. His chest rises and falls, but there is a lot of blood on him. Too much. I find a large bite missing from the back of his neck.

Ripping the shirt off the back of a nearby corpse, I wad it and press it to the wound. "We need to get him to your infirmary. I think he'll be okay."

"Biting doesn't turn him into..."the skinny soldier trails off.

"No," I say with a chuckle. "The virus is in the air. We're all breathing it right now. He'll just have a really bad scar and anemia."

"I'm John, by the way," the scrawny soldier says as he lifts his comrade by the shoulders. "This is Dave."

“Volunteers to take Dave to the infirmary and cover them?” I look at the group behind me. One of the girls comes forward and takes Dave’s feet. Two boys with rifles, including Brian, follow them, guns ready.

“Everyone else, let’s see what we can carry.” I grin as I walk into the warehouse, eager to do some shopping.

A couple hours later, I’m tossing a grenade ahead of me. I’m not even sure there are meat sacks in the room, but every other barracks had at least one. Heph waits for me to get my barrel up before opening the door again, and charging in. The metal bunk frames are relatively unscathed, a few char marks. The mattresses are toast, but we’ve already found a room full of those. We also find a meat sack, pushing himself up with one hand, the other and matching leg both gone. I put a bullet through his head before he gets any ideas.

“Clear,” Heph shouts from the other side, not phased at all by the corpse lying a foot from where he stands. Much more trusting than my

Heph, this one let the animal touch him, knowing I would shoot it. "Just the one this time. How many more?"

I consult a map that John sent us after getting Dave settled in the infirmary. "Looks like that's the last. I don't know. I think we should do another circuit. There might be some hiding outside."

"Cassy, it's getting dark and we've checked outside twice. Joshua, Nathan, and Dan have been circling too. I think that's all of them."

I sigh and let my rifle hang by the strap on my shoulder. "You're right. I'm just paranoid. Let's show the girls where the mattresses are and start setting this place up for the night."

"Brian already did that," Heph tells me. Brian brought us the map, then set about helping us clean house. "Take a break, Cass."

He leads me to a bench outside and takes my hand as he sits.

"What about the board? Has the news gone out?" I ask, referring to our website.

Heph sighs and pulls on my arm hard. I fall into him, banging our heads together.

"Ow!" I grab my forehead.

He links his ankles together around the back of my legs, wraps arms around my torso. "Relax. You don't have to do everything. We got the message. Then we got the message out. I think there are already a few carloads from Denver."

Hearing that, I do relax. "They're coming."

He nods and his head moves against mine, already it's less oily than before. "That's right. You did it, Cassy."

I sink into him, my head falling into the curve of his neck. "Thank you."

"For what?" he asks, brushing a hand through my hair.

"For believing me. For being here."

"Thank you for coming for me." He kisses my forehead and I close my eyes, feeling safe enough to sleep.

Freetown.

Chapter Five

ESTABLISHING FREETOWN is harder than I expected, harder than the first time. There are so many of us, so many non-combatants. We have children, younger than six, and school kids up to sixteen. I wouldn't let any of them face a meat sack alone.

In addition to those I wouldn't ask to fight are those who refuse to fight. Most of the girls, like me the first time, are too scared to pick up a gun and point it at a person. The few that are willing practice marksmanship and martial arts with

Heph and others. The rest, well, we have a lot of kids to look after. Some girls balk at that duty as well. I've already lost it on six or seven of them. There are no free rides here. Either you train and help raid, or you take care of Freetown and everyone in it.

Speaking of raids, I plan the first a week after taking Fort Carson and establishing Freetown. Calling a general meeting, I gather everyone that is over sixteen, except three girls minding the children. Several boys under sixteen, but thankfully over twelve, gathered with the others. I pretend not to notice them. They aren't going alone. I can look the other way.

"I need volunteers," I announce.

Six or seven hands go up immediately and I snicker slightly. Some of the boys have gotten more than a little antsy over the last week.

"Yes, yes, I see you. I'm actually looking for a few ladies to join our party."

Most of the girls shuffle and avoid my eye.

"I'm looking for shoppers."

That gets their attention.

"I need four teams. Each team will have two guards and three raiders." Twenty people. That's about a third of our current 'over sixteen' population. I'm hoping for more over the week. Taking my worry off informing people, I focus on the task at hand: raiding. "The guards surround the vehicle, keeping the meat sacks off as long as possible. The raiders are my shoppers. Normally I'd just take more guards, people who can help keep the sacks off." The guys, who have been attending combat practice, nod and look at one another smugly. I try not to think about how many will probably fall in their first raid. Training is great, but nothing really prepares you for a meat sack that takes a shot to the gut and just keeps on coming.

"As many of you are aware, the army doesn't carry much in smaller sizes." I nod my head toward the kids playing in another part of the yard. "Normally raiders set their sights on food, anything non-perishable. These next few raids, however, are for supplies. I want warm clothing, shoes, boots and coats. Grab some baby clothes while you're there." We don't have any actual infants, but I'm still hopeful. Also, assuming we survive nine months, we're probably going to have new babies before we really want to think about it.

"What about toys?" someone asks.

There is some scoffing, but I nod. "A little. Don't take time on it. If the meat sacks are on your door, you split. If you've filled three carts with clothes and they still aren't after you, yeah, a few toys for the kids would probably be a good thing." Not for the first time, I wish we hadn't had to drop a grenade in the common room. The Xbox and games were toast. Instead, they've been entertaining themselves, but I imagine there are only so many buildings you can make out of empty ammo casings before you need a new thing. "Make sure you get things that last: Lego, puzzles, board games. No Nerf or anything requiring batteries. By the way, grab batteries," I add as an afterthought.

I earn a few snickers for that, too. Hell, I don't care, I'm not a born leader and I only have a half-assed idea of what I'm doing.

"I'm coming on the first raid as a raider, so after I will have a better shopping list. We're going to hit the Wal-Mart." A hand goes up in the back, but I ignore it. "They've got a little bit of everything. We'll load our vehicle with all it can hold until the sacks clue in to us. Then we plow our way out."

"Isn't that stealing?" the girl in the back shouts. "I mean, we all locked our stores in the mall so no one could loot them."

I chuckle wryly. "Who do you think is going to come looking for the stuff here? Who is going to arrest us? Who is going to use the goods in those stores if we don't? We're all there is, folks. It's us and the brain dead. Do you think they want the kids' clothes?"

Several guys up front laugh with me.

"Is it stealing?" I ask. "Yeah, it is. We didn't make those things and we didn't do anything to get them, but we're also the only ones who can claim them. If they belonged to a corporation, that company doesn't exist anymore. If they belonged to a shop owner, he probably doesn't exist anymore. No one owns anything. Let me say that again, louder. No one owns anything! Not anymore. What we have is for the good of the survivors and belongs to all of us. If we survive long enough to actually start a new way of life, an economy and stuff like that, we'll revisit the issue of ownership. As long as it's a fight for our lives, we use what we have."

There are a number of grumbles from the oldest in the group. I ignore them. If they want to lead, all they have to do is step up.

"So, volunteers," I say again, rubbing my hands. "Who wants to go on a shopping spree?"

I only get three girls so I put them each on a different team. I have more than enough boys and contemplate taking six, but the bodies in the van cut down on how much we can bring back. At noon, the next day, I assemble my team. I want to take Heph, but at the same time I think it would be better to balance the teams, and he is a strong guard. That's how I end up in a green van with four boys I barely know. They are all decent shots, at least. I let Nick, the bulkiest of my party, drive and can't help laughing as he pulls into a parking spot.

"Dude. No one is going to tow us. Park right at the door. If you can, back it in. Hey, wait! They have an auto bay here!" How did I not notice that the first time?

"Yeah, don't all Wal-Marts?" one of the other boys answers.

"Pull into there. If we're out of sight, we might not attract attention."

"Sure, Seeress," Nick replies. "You got the magic door opener?"

Chuckling, I slide open the side door. "I think I do." Automatic off, I love my army issue rifle, I put a single bullet through the customer service door and run inside.

I keep my gun up, glad I do as a pair of meat sacks rush me. By the smell, they weren't the only shoppers trapped inside as everyone fell to the virus. Holding my breath slightly, I squeeze out single shots, taking each adult in the middle of the forehead. Neither body will be getting up again, pinkish spray exiting the back of their heads. Not enough brain left. Keeping my attention on the store, I back myself to the service counter and peek over it.

There is half of a body on the floor and a puddle of dried blood with insects stuck in it. The first time, a sight like that would have me blowing chunks. I've seen so many corpses now that I barely blink, only registering that the head is gone. This sack isn't moving again, victim of his fellows.

Swinging my rifle in one more arc, I let it fall to my side and heave myself onto the counter, my legs falling on the other side. I land wide of the sticky puddle, wrinkling my nose as I pass into the automotive bay.

The power doors aren't working, but the chain works fine, letting me pull the door up long enough for the van to pull in.

"Are you okay?" Nick asks. "Luke and Mark followed you." Those are the two wiry ones that are raiding with me. I hear retching and assume that's the boys.

"I'm fine, just a pair of sacks. Keep the keys in the ignition." I rub my hands in glee. "I'm going shopping!"

Nick laughs, but he and Vince are the guards, staying with the van. I trot back to the counter and pretend not to notice the fresh vomit on the floor. I lift the segment of counter, it's much easier to see from this side, and meet up with the boys.

"Take a cart. On your marks, get set. Go!" I yell, grabbing one of the blue plastic carts and pushing off, jumping on the back to sail through the wide corridor toward the children's section. There is some clatter, and over my shoulder I see Mark and Luke pulling their own carts and wheeling away in different directions. One heads to the groceries, the other the pharmacy.

Hopping off the back of the cart, I walk up to a rack of long sleeved t-shirts for boys. Scooping the whole set off its metal arm, I drop it in the cart. Girls, boys, large, small, I need everything and versatility wins out over fashion. The girls won't get dresses and some boys might be wearing pink parkas, but I'm sure I have a little of everything from size three to fourteen. Anyone older and bigger than that gets army fatigues for the time being.

Punching the pile down in the cart, I turn to shoes, planning to grab kids, ladies, and men's boots. The army boots are fine, but the basics aren't really ideal for snow, as I recall. Of course, being summer, there aren't a lot of boots on the shelves.

Gunshots ring out and I wheel my cart with only a handful of pairs of boots. I toss the last ones atop the rest and sprint toward automotive. Mark and Luke are each there already, their carts not quite full. They have their rifles out and are firing into the mob of meat sacks breaking through the garage door.

"Damn," I curse, "they smelled us." I shouldn't be surprised. Switching my safety off and automatic on, I rain bullets into the crowd with the others. Nick and Vince are trapped with their backs to the van. I walk behind Mark and Luke, who are obviously overwhelmed, and fire as I strafe toward the other side of the van. The meat sacks are beginning to circle it and I push a little faster, putting my rifle right in the eye of the nearest to push him away from the driver's door.

One more arc and I twist a hand behind me to open the unlocked van. I kick out, hitting a sack in the chin before slamming the door shut again. My rifle falls to my side, and I reach out for the keys, turning them sharply.

The engine grinds and I grin. Nick left it running. Honking once, I toss the van in reverse, knowing that Nick and Vince are probably going to get clocked by the side-view mirror, but it's the best way short of explosives to take out this many sacks. Churning them under my tires, I back up until I hit the remains of the garage door. Through the windshield, I see more meat sacks and four boys falling beneath them.

I honk again and the boys jump as much as they're able to the side, dragging the most persistent creatures with them. I swing close on the right, trying to clip monsters and not men. The boys kick and pull, but I notice there are only three of them now. The side door opens and with a crash the two wiry boys land on the floor in the back. Pointing my rifle out the open door, I wait for the third. Nick has Vince on his shoulder as he struggles into the van.

"Close that door!" I shout, jamming the van into reverse again. "We're out of here."

This has to be the least successful raid I've ever led.

"What happened?" I cry out, speeding through Carson back to the fort. "Where did they all come from?"

There is panting and groaning from the back. Nick just shrugs his wide shoulders. "Dunno. Everywhere."

"Did you time us? Did we take too long?"

He's not really looking at me, but I can see his shaggy brown head in the rearview as he shakes it. I can also see Mark and Luke moving a little, Vince not at all. "You'd been out six minutes, I think."

Six minutes. What did I do wrong?

"Could you not yell at us right now, Cassy?" Mark asks, holding his head. "I think my ears are ringing."

Sighing quietly, I try not to blame inexperience. "Okay. No yelling," I agree. "How is Vince?"

"The bleeding isn't bad. He just went down when the mirror clipped him," Nick explains.

I grunt, predicting that.

"Heh," Luke chuckles. "He's going to have a goose egg there."

"As long as he's okay," I mutter. "Next time, Nick?" His head comes up to meet my eyes in the mirror. "Don't leave the van. It's your biggest and best weapon."

His smile is weak. "Yeah, you wield it well."

I chuckle in return. "Thanks."

***

After the first disastrous run at Wal-Mart, the other three go smoothly. Go figure. The place is pretty empty by the time the fourth group goes through. They bring back a ton of games and paper and pens for the kids to play with. I can't find the heart to be upset about that.

Smashing the glass of the third and final grocery store left in Fort Carson, Heph and I hurry into the maze of aisles like rats after the cheese. I get cheese. I also load up on butter and milk. The milk is probably all spoiled, but there might be a few cartons in the back that haven't turned.

Heph has found cheese too, but already baked into buns and bread. Like my selections, there might be some spoilage, but we'll take what we can carry and sort it out at the other end.

We leave our carts with the crew at the van. Raids have become much safer since the first disaster. Three guards and two raiders, instead of the other way around, seems to be working better. The guards are already opening fire on the meat sacks coming our way, but we hurry for one more pass. It's dangerous, but we'd rather not have to come back. The meat sacks will probably pull the place apart after we go. This time we hit staples:

flour, rice, sugar. I've got the baking aisle, tossing sack after sack of sugar and flour. There is a crashing of metal an aisle over as Heph sweeps cans from shelves.

Sprinting for the truck, we both pull our pistols and fire with the guard at the van. Another refinement, a rifle really slows down a raider.

"Do it, Cass," Heph tells me and I stash my gun, throwing sacks into the back. Heph and another of the guard cease fire to lift his cart and pour tin cans atop the flour and sugar. I'm already climbing atop the pile, as is one other guard. Then Heph jumps in, yanking the doors as the last two hop into the front and peel out, crushing zombies beneath our tires.

It's not like they were eating the food anyway.

Theft, property, and law in general are all absent in this new world. We police ourselves, somewhat. Certainly the first time, there was hardly any order. It isn't the same this time. There are so many more of us, and we are able to loot so much more. Already the oldest among us are banding together to provide some sort of leadership. Nothing like that happened last time, the first time. This time we do have a sense of ownership over our salvaged personal items, of the items we loot. Not this food, that's obviously for everyone, but I see one of the guards grabbed a magazine from the racks near the tills. I bet he doesn't share that.

It's odd. There weren't as many meat sacks in the attack this time as I would have expected. Every beating heart within a mile will come to the smell of fresh meat. They're feeding on each other at this point and between that and our firepower, they might actually be dying out. I told Heph that couldn't happen, and it can't, not really, but this population of zombies might be wiped out entirely. We might have the rest of town to live in instead of just the base. We could use the extra space.

Unfortunately, this means we'll be ranging farther for supplies in the future. Based on the number of people we're supplying, that'll be sooner rather than later. Longer raids are inevitability more dangerous.

I yawn and I'm not alone. Some, like me, have taken to sleeping during the day, preferring to be alert in the dark. Almost anyone who has had a meat sack sneak up on them during a raid or on their way to Freetown is the same way. We can't have light all night long, that would waste what precious gas and diesel we have, but we can wear infrared goggles.

The gates of the base open for us and close as soon as we arrive. Six boys with guns surround the gate, making sure nothing follows us in. Surprisingly, none of the meat sacks have. They're stupid but will usually follow the trail. Only one shot fires and I look out to see the dog that lies in the road.

Animals are easily as dangerous as the mindless humans. I suppose their young would be like us, but they age even faster than we do, so it seems like they're all flesh eaters. Thinking about it reminds me of Jay. We'd had to evict him from Freetown the first time when he came down with a fever and delusions. He'd just turned twenty.

We jump out of the back of the van as a group of people come to unload and sort it. I get out of the way. I'm not one who deals with our supplies and haven't been since drawing up the original shopping lists. These days, I just grab what they tell me. Heph steadies me when I wobble, fighting another huge yawn.

"Let's get you to your bunk," he says, keeping a hand around my waist.

"And your interest in my . . ." another yawn, "fatigue has nothing to do with . . ." yawn, "watching me undress."

"Nothing whatsoever," he says with a remarkably straight face. I can't help but laugh. "Hell, you don't have to undress, just take off your boots. That's how you sleep most days, isn't it?"

My brow furrows. "Have you been spying on me?" My bunk mates are all female and most don't sleep during the day.

He has the decency to blush. "Maybe a little, just through the window. Also, we came here together, remember? I see how on edge you are when there's even the possibility of a meat sack nearby. I'm surprised you don't sleep with a gun."

A yawn again as we enter the empty barracks. The only person in it is Denise and she's passed out on top of the covers. I'm more than ready to join her in dreamland. I remove my belt and hold onto one of the knives while the other falls with the belt. "Too dangerous. I almost shot off my arm once." I slide the knife under my pillow and then flop down.

Heph looks a little surprised. "You sleep with a knife under your pillow?"

"Uh-huh," I grunt around another yawn. "Don't you? You used to." I'm blinking heavily, barely conscious now that I'm on the mattress. "Shit, sorry, I keep forgetting you're not like him. Don't mean to compare." I roll over and grab at the blankets at my feet.

Heph pulls one over me and kisses my cheek. "Don't worry about it. I just don't believe I was ever that badass. Not like you."

"Mmm, you were more badass, way more badass. You were amazing, and you let me follow you around until I could keep up. You were the best. You are the best, Heph. I love you."

"You're dead to the world, Cassy. Tell me that when I can believe you."

"Okay," I murmur drowsily. If I say anything else, I'm not aware of it.

CHAPTER SIX

DESPITE THE much larger population arriving, I'm still at the gate every time the rumbling of a vehicle approaches. I like having my own tally for the population of Freetown. Every one that is over five hundred feels like a victory to me. That's why I am nearby when Jenny's bus pulls in.

Jenny and Heph are easily the two people I miss the most. Although I have Heph back, he isn't the same as my Heph, the first Heph. Jenny, however, should be pretty much the same. She should still be the pregnant girl who can cook for fifty while rocking a crying kid to sleep. She should still be unwilling to touch a gun, forget about firing one.

I see her through one of the front windows of the bus, blond hair being yanked by the child with her, and I jump aboard as soon as the doors open. Rushing forward, I wrap her in a hug.

“Uh, do I know you?” Jenny asks, hugging me back.

“Not this time, but you did.”

“You’re Cassandra!” she says in a shriek, tightening her hold again. “Thank you for warning us. All the daycares were attacked. We got some of them.” She chokes up a little and one of the girls with her hugs her shoulders and whispers to Jenny.

“Did you lose any?”

Jenny nods, tears spilling over. “Dylan. I think he’s...“

She turns to look back and I see a pair of boots sticking out from the only seat without heads over it. Releasing Jenny, I move toward him. He has a bloody cloth around his shoulder and upper arm, but it is obviously dried blood. His chest rises and falls steadily. I lift one of his heels and let it drop back to the seat.

"Wha? Ow!" His cry turns to a groan as he holds his head.

"I think he's fine," I assure Jenny, slipping past her and another older girl to jump down the bus steps. "We need a stretcher," I call to the boys on guard.

"You got it, Seeress."

Closing my eyes and gritting my teeth, I shout, "It's Cassy!" Being Seeress was kinda cool for a week, but I'm really getting tired of it. Pulling myself up by the bus rail, I land toe-to-toe with Jenny. The toddler tugging her hair is now on her hip. "Don't worry. There's a med student here. He'll take care of him." Ken, one of the few people besides Jenny and Heph that I remember from the first time, arrived with the first carloads from Denver.

Jenny still looks overwhelmed and I hug her, taking the little boy from her.

"You did great," I tell her with enthusiasm. "The first time, the youngest of us was four and the next after that was six. Siblings. But you, you brought us all sorts of kids. Orphans?" I ask.

Jenny nods. "Yes. Many of these are siblings, but they don't have parents or older sibs to look after them. You really did this once before? Did you know?" She rubs her belly which doesn't even have a bump yet to show. In fact, I bet if I lift her shirt, I'll see ribs. She's as skinny as I remember. The baby, when she did show, looked like its own growth, not matching the rest of her slight frame.

I hesitate in answering. My knowledge of the future is next to useless now, but some things will still apply. "Yes, but so much has changed. I've met your baby though, and that's all I'm willing to say about it." Patience had only been six weeks old when I died, so mostly I remembered her asleep.

"I see." She gets a thoughtful look that is lost when we hear the whimpering of children in the back of the bus. "How are we taking care of the children?" She follows me out of the bus and looks around the compound. "I like the base. It's good to share living space." She looks past me to the barracks.

"It is. We haven't cleaned up all the barracks, although we're probably going to run out of mattresses. I'm sure we can find something in town."

"You go out?" she asks in alarm. "You fight them?"

Dylan is carried out behind us as we walk toward one of the administration buildings. The boys with the stretcher jog past us to the medic station.

I smile wryly. "Yes, but you won't have to. Stay here, look after the little ones. There are enough of us to watch the edges and go on raids. These kids should have nothing to worry about. And what is your name, little man?" I ask, slipping my finger into his tiny fist.

"This is Gabriel. He's only ten months old. I brought all the formula we had in the daycare, but we'll need more of that, and diapers."

I can't help but grin. The first time, I wouldn't think of things like that until the last diaper needed to be changed. As it was, I didn't expect children this small. We will have to raid for diapers. "Let me introduce you to John. He's our...procurement manager." I give the title somewhat facetiously. Of the five eldest, John is organizing both the people and time of raids as well as what we are going to get.

Jenny falls in beside me as I lead the way through the base, pointing out different areas and how we're using them. I stop at the boardroom and knock on the door. Stephanie, the oldest female among us, opens it a crack. There are a group of five that are over twenty. They have taken over running Freetown, to my relief and satisfaction.

"Yes, Cassandra?"

"This is Jenny. She just arrived with over forty young children, including infants. She'd like to talk to John about special items for them."

Stephanie smiles a little. She's so stiff that it looks uncomfortable even though it's probably genuine. "Of course, come in, Jenny."

I leave Jenny with the eldest and return to help the rest of her group find a place to settle in. They'll probably need an entire barracks of their own, assuming that those who came want to work with the little ones. I know I wouldn't. I'm thrilled to see them, I want them here for what they mean for continued existence, but I don't want to change a diaper. My nose wrinkles at the thought.

"Bad egg?" Heph asks. He falls in beside me, his rifle ever-present. I'm not usually without mine, but I'd just woken when the bus arrived. We usually work the perimeter together, but the schedule changes when new people are added and some find they can't handle shooting something that looks human.

"Nah. We got a busload of babies and I was thinking about diapers." Heph's nose wrinkles as I expect mine just did. "Yes, exactly."

"Who's going to babysit?" he asks.

I shrug. "The people who don't want to fight. There are enough of those that they can take turns."

We insisted everyone over twelve learn to shoot a gun, in case we are ever overrun. However, no one is required to carry or even use one again after that first lesson. Guns are only given to kids over sixteen, but it's important that the younger ones know how to pick up a fallen rifle or pistol. A lot of older girls and no few boys opt not to take guard duty or help on raids. This time, there are enough of us that there are hundreds of other things to do: laundry, cooking, cleaning, organizing supplies, first aid, and now babysitting. Everyone has been able to find something that helps the group.

"A busload. They actually brought a bus?" Heph asks.

I nod and lead him toward where the long yellow vehicle is parked. Since we've been here, Heph has been studying mechanics with David who happened to be in the engineer corps. I know what he really wants to see isn't the bus, but its engine.

While he tinkers, I take a moment to admire his backside. It's gotten tighter with all the work outs and marching. Then I look around the base at the chaos that is Freetown. People mill everywhere. Many have things to do but are in no rush to do them. It is so different from the first time. As I watch, I see one boy shove another into the dirt. Bullying isn't uncommon and there isn't a lot to be done about it. There isn't a formal structure, just those who are older and younger. It's likely that one boy was older than the one he pushed. I could, being older than either, step in, but they'd just be at it again as soon as I left.

I'm not sure I like Freetown this time. It's good that so many people escaped, found somewhere to go, but I don't like us all in one place. It feels like a bomb about to explode.

"Sweet," Heph says, pulling me from less than happy thoughts.

"What?" I ask.

"Same engine as the army buses. We have spare parts." He grins and sweeps long black strands from his eyes.

"You should really cut that," I remind him.

"Why? It's not like I can't see."

"I don't know. It just seems dangerous."

"I thought you liked me dangerous," he teases, wrapping hands around my waist and pulling me closer. His fingers play over my ribs as he leans down to place his nose within reach of mine.

His acne is gone, leaving only a few marks of its existence. His blue eyes bore into me, making me shake very slightly. I close my eyes as he leans closer yet.

"Cassy and Jonah, sitting in a tree!"

I groan and step away.

"Where'd you hear that name? I'm Heph!" Heph shakes a fist at the boy, scaring him off. He can't be more than eight or nine.

I bite my lip to keep from laughing. "He probably heard John call you that, sorry." I would have expected the army soldier to take to last names, but John is pretty insistent on calling people by their first or middle names; maybe because we aren't part of any families to use family names. It won't change me; I'll always call him Heph.

"Where are the ankle biters?" Heph asks, leaning on the side of the bus.

"Sixth barracks. I think they'll all fit in one. We'll see. I'm on shift soon. You?"

He shakes his head. "We've got a raid this afternoon."

"I didn't hear about a raid."

"Yeah, John dropped it on us this morning."

"At least he didn't ask you to go at sunset."

Heph doesn't say anything, but he doesn't meet my gaze either.

"What could possibly be important enough to go outside the perimeter after dark?" I ask, my voice gaining pitch with every word.

Heph shrugs. "I just follow the boss." He shifts uneasily from foot to foot. The first time, he was the boss. I'm starting to wonder if I made more mistakes than assuming that killing the doctor would kill the virus.

"I'm going to find out." I start marching the way I came, back to the boardroom where I left Jenny.

I find her standing outside, soothing Gabriel. "Shh. I know the big man sounded scary. You're okay, sweetie."

"Need any help?" I ask, praying the answer is no.

"Not really. Sounds like they're going to plan for those supplies soon. They were surprised by how many kids I brought."

"I'll bet," I answer with a grin. "Pleasantly, I hope."

Jenny's face falls a little. "I'm not sure. First was plain shock, but then everyone stayed really quiet. Finally, Stephanie assured me that the supplies would be found. I'm glad canned and powdered formula lasts forever." She rubs her belly for a moment.

"She giving you trouble?" I ask, reaching tentatively toward the unborn without actually touching Jenny.

"No." She looks down to her hand, but then snaps her head up to meet my gaze. "She?"

I sigh quietly. I suppose it won't hurt to tell her what I knew. "Yes, a baby girl. She'll be born in November. You named her Patience."

"Patience," Jenny murmurs. Shifting her hold on Gabriel, she links with my elbow. "So, I have the feeling you and I will be friends."

I chuckle quietly. "We were, yes. I'd like to be again."

"I'm pretty sure we already are."

***

The rest of Freetown is sleeping around us. Heph asked me to join him on the perimeter, even though neither of us are on patrol tonight.

"What's up?" I ask, taking his hand.

"This," he says and points up. Just as he does a streak flashes across the sky. "They'll pick up in the next hour."

"What are they?" I ask. He sits on a blanket he's laid out on the ground. I join him and we both lie back.

"Meteor shower. There's one every August."

I try to remember ever seeing it before and can't. I suppose I never took the time. I remember hearing about them, but never sitting outside to watch. "It's beautiful," I tell him. "Thank you." I roll to my side, letting one leg drape over him.

"Thank you for sharing it with me. My family almost always goes camping so we can see them without the city lights." He laughs and I have to join him. The only lights now are run on our diesel generator, so we don't use them unless we have to. The patrols use the infrared goggles that were in storage rather than flashlights. They're especially good at spotting the fever hot meat sacks. Unfortunately, they often pick up feverish rodents and cattle, too. Everything is rabid and flesh-eating.

"Where did you go?" I've heard a lot of stories about his family, but I'm eager to hear more, too.

"Around. Last year we went to Yellowstone, year before was the Grand Canyon. What about you?"

I shake my head before resting it on his shoulder. "My family likes the beach. We go to California at least once every summer, usually two or three times. Mom's from the coast and misses it. I like it too, the surf and sand." I think about awaking on the beach to find I had a chance to undo everything. Even though I wasn't as successful as I'd hoped, I'm still thrilled with what I did accomplish this time. People are sleeping on the floors of barracks, there are so many of us; easily four or five times as many people as the first time.

"The beach is okay, I guess. I like the mountains." He grins. "I wasn't exactly sad when you told me Freetown was in Colorado."

I chuckle, too. The mountains are just outside our door. "I'll admit to being a little concerned about winter here. I packed everything warm I own, but I'm pretty sure it still isn't going to be enough when it snows here, and the stores aren't carrying the really heavy stuff at this time of year."

"Yeah, snow," Heph doesn't sound intimidated, rather wistful. "I wish we got snow more often."

I grimace. One of the things I like best about New Mexico and a reason I miss it is the lack of snow. "Well, you'll get your wish. There'll be snow in November."

He stiffens for a moment and then relaxes. "I don't think I'll ever get used to that. You know, when all the cold snaps come, don't you?"

I shiver at the memory. "Yes. I hated them."

"And unlike some things, the weather won't change."

I yawn, the day catching up with me. "That's right. Every day I remember rain from the first time, it's rained again. Why?"

"Nothing. Just makes you a little less approachable, y'know?"

"No, I don't know," I snapped. "I'm just me."

"You're the girl who has lived all this before. You say I'm the one that taught you how to fight, but I'm following your example. You're not only armed with combat skills, serious ones, but knowledge. You know when and where some things happen. I'm just...Why would you want to hang out with me?"

I sigh. He doesn't understand. "Because I need you, Heph. I know you aren't the same boy that taught me Aikido or Jujitsu. You're not the Heph that put a gun in my hand and told me the best way to learn was to use it. You aren't the boy I fell in love with."

I'm not surprised when he starts to shift away from me. I don't let him, gripping his shoulders.

"You are the boy who believed me when I started spouting nonsense at him. None of my friends did. They all thought I was crazy. You came with me when I suggested the insane capture of a military base. You are the Heph that's here, and I love you as much as I love him. I think no less of you and you trust me more."

"Well, I have to. You're the only person making sense most of the time. I think all these kids would still be spinning in circles if you hadn't pulled them together."

I frown at the memory. “That’s exactly what most of them did. Then we, volunteers from Freetown, had to go find the few who had managed to hide and survive. Not an easy job, and not a safe one either. That was how I died.”

There’s silence for a few minutes while we both watch the sky become streaked with meteors.

“Tell me how you died?” Heph asked.

I shudder, not wanting to remember. “We were on a search and rescue. Everyone was pretty sure there were cells in the larger centers, and you and I were sent east to find as many as we could carry back. You were inside one of the unburned buildings while I guarded outside. For some reason, I can’t remember now, we didn’t bring enough ammunition, so I was armed with my knives.”

Heph sucks a breath through his teeth. He knows that wouldn’t be good if we were attacked in any numbers.

“I heard them coming and struck. I wasn’t even really frightened, just annoyed I didn’t have a gun. One managed to get near enough to bite me and took my neck.”

Heph flinches this time.

“I didn’t feel much; only a painful snapping. Then I was on the beach with my parents again, eight months earlier.” I shrug, my shoulder moving against his. “I didn’t believe it at first, thought maybe I was in a strange form of hell, but I wasn’t. I was in my own past with a chance to change things.”

Heph rolls towards me, propping up on an elbow. “I know you think you should have done more, but look at what you managed. How many people are here that weren’t the first time? You’re amazing, Cassy.” He leans in and I press my lips to his. The kiss stays chaste only a moment or two. Heph hesitates but follows my lead, his hands running over and under my shirt. I love feeling his hands on me. He has long nimble fingers that hold a Glock steady or cup my breast and hip. His hair has grown long in the last month and tickles my cheek, but I don’t brush it back.

My hands are already reaching into the back of his jeans, pulling him closer to me.

"God, could you pick a better place?" someone shouts at us, probably one of the patrols. I huddle in on myself trying to cover anything Heph had managed to expose. He's gotten my shirt off and my bra is skewed. I straighten it before crossing my arms.

Heph just laughs. "Oh, get lost. You know there isn't anywhere else."

"Yeah, there's a reason for that." Something small lands in the grass next to us. A condom. "We have enough of those that you'd better be using one," the disembodied voice threatens.

I squint, trying to make out a face, but can barely make out the smudge against the dark that is his outline.

I can see Heph's face in the star and moonlight. He's disappointed and tries to pull my arms apart, kissing the top of my chest. Fumbling, he gets his hand on the condom and draws the corner down my arm, making me shiver.

"No, Heph, not here, not tonight." I try to snag the condom, but he just slides it into his back pocket.

"Okay. Lots of other things we can do." His lips continue to roam my body. I arch my back and look up into the star-streaked sky. It seems I've opened Pandora's box. All I can think is, why didn't we do this the first time?

***

"Cassy? Are you busy?"

I'm surprised that the answer is no. Was there any free time the first time? Not that I can recall. "No. What's up, Jenny?"

She sits on the bunk beside me, pulling her blond hair back and twisting it. "I need to talk to someone."

"Is it about the baby?" I ask, curious.

"No, no. That's fine. It's about Adam."

Adam. There are about four Adams our age. "Which one?"

"Oh, you didn't meet him."

"Is he . . ." I stare at her belly, curious. I know nothing about the father of her baby. She didn't tell me and I never asked.

She still isn't showing, as skinny as ever. I know I'm not chunky or anything, but Jenny is a rail. I remember wondering how she cooked so well if she didn't eat, until I watched her eat. She just doesn't store anything, apparently.

"No," she says again, sighing. "He was twelve."

I blink. That's unexpected. Now I'm really curious who Adam is.

"He had two sisters, Penny and Violet."

Those names I recognize. "Oh, yeah, they came with you."

Jenny nods and her blue-green eyes fill with tears. "He came, too. Well, he tried to come with us. We had the bus by then, and with so many of us, they started chasing."

I nod in understanding.

"The bus wasn't even half full. I had plans to go to three other day cares, but they just wouldn't let us." She choked up. "Adam pushed Penny through the open doors and I caught her hand, pulling her up while we drove on."

Not sure what I should do, I wrap one arm around Jenny's shoulders. "And you got away."

Jenny shakes her head. "Violet was still running. Violet was the younger of the pair, no more than seven. She tripped and fell."

I cover my mouth as I gasp. The meat sacks chasing would have fallen on her like flies on rotting meat.

"I don't know how she survived," Jenny says. "I just know that Adam pulled her up and shoved her after the bus. She stumbled and caught the stair rail, her feet dragging along as she tried to pull herself up. But she was too small. She cried for Adam, but he...the mob swarmed over him."

I close my eyes and tighten my hold on Jenny.

She starts babbling as she hurries on. "We slowed down to help Violet up, and I was looking out the door as I took her hand. They tore him apart, Cassy. Ripped his arms right—" She stops, a gurgling sound in her throat. She's going to be sick, I'm sure. I yank the wastebasket out and into her hands just in time.

"I'm so sorry, Jenny. I'm sorry you couldn't save him."

She puts the basket down and starts crying into her hands, her bony shoulders shaking. "They all stopped chasing and we used that to stop at another day care. We were able to get everyone on bus before they finished—" Jenny can't finish, her tears lining her cheeks. "When they came back, they had bits of his clothes stuck to their faces." She shudders, holding herself even as I try to hold her. "It is still the worst thing I've ever seen."

I take a moment to inhale slowly, exhaling in a huff. "I wish that were the worst I've seen." I've watched a boy scream and claw at his own neck to try to tear free of a meat sack. I've watched them pull a head free, far bloodier than an arm. No, the worst was probably watching one suck up intestines like spaghetti from a torso still squirting blood.

Snatching the basket, I deposit my dinner next to Jenny's.

"Are you okay?" she asks, wiping her mouth with the back of a hand.

I nod weakly. "Yeah. Stay in the fort," I tell her. "Make sure you never see worse." I push myself off the bunk, eager to find someone to practice with. I have some serious rage to work out.

"Cassy," Jenny calls when I reach the door. "Thank you for listening."

I smile thinly. "Anytime. If you have any more nightmares you need to let out, find me."

"I will," she says with a little more volume, a little steadier.

I hurry off to find Heph. I want a good fight.

CHAPTER SEVEN

FREETOWN IS even more chaotic than I remember. The few of us that survived didn't need organization before, but it's quickly obvious that without someone planning a meal well in advance, no one is going to get to eat. Jenny is quick to step into that role. She finds a few other teens who have worked in various restaurants to help her.

Jenny is as amazing as the first time. She's sporting a definite baby bump as she marches young adults and children alike around the compound, organizing them into classes. Almost every time I see her, I wrap her up in a hug, catching a baby in her carrier between us. Technically, Patience, her daughter, is between us as well. We're even closer this time, if that's possible. It's likely because there are so many of us that cliques are inevitable. I'm in hers. Period. Heph can be in it too.

She asks me often about her pregnancy and birthing. I know she's scared, and I can assure her that the first time, everything went smoothly. I don't tell her how long her labor was. I'm hoping it isn't as long this time for one reason or another. In any case, she doesn't need to know contractions were constant for over twenty hours. I wish I didn't know that.

We also talk about town, about how crowded things are. Jenny doesn't mind sticking two or three kids in a bed—she finds they sleep better with company. No, her concern is about the older kids, the way they rotate bunks. I spend most nights on patrol and sleep during the day, crashing on a mattress that someone just rose from. When I wake in eight hours, a third person will take it. If I don't wake in eight hours, she'll be shaking me awake, wanting her bed. Even rotating like that, three to a bed, we're running out of mattresses and places to sleep.

Child supervision shouldn't be a problem, not with a new car or bus arriving full of survivors desperate for a place to stay every few days. Only the daycare workers and a few others are willing to look after little kids for more than a couple hours at a time. Everyone is bored. Even though Freetown is bursting from the seams and we're doing constant raids, there still doesn't seem to be enough to keep everyone busy. We range farther and farther afield to get enough food and fuel to keep us running, but there are always more people staying behind than go out.

The leaders are trying to deal with it. They aren't turning people away, but something is going to give. One or more seam is bursting.

We are a bunch of kids, so it's not surprising that bullying is rampant in Freetown, making it safe only for the littlest ones. Anyone else might be beat up for their food, their blankets, anything the bully can find worth taking. The council put a stop to the first rape gang, but I expect there are others. So many boys and so few girls. We'd been safe the first time because everyone learned how to fight and no one was alone. This time, there are many kids with no assigned task, no partner for scary nights and bleak days. The council believes they are establishing some sort of order, but it is a thin and fragile thing. It only adds to my desire to get out of here.

I've suggested expanding into the city. We should be able to eradicate enough meat sacks to extend the perimeter. The biggest problem will be building a new wall or fence. The compound is perfect that way, with electric fencing. We should be able to extend the same fence and the same power source, but no one is planning to do anything.

I'm bouncing ideas off Jenny and Heph. Both can see the same things I do, the growing tension and lack of supplies. Few return from each raid, fewer than left. They notice the perimeter breaches that are always close to the nurseries.

Heph is on board with my plan. He's the one who suggests finding another base instead of extending this one. It makes sense. There won't be any military left in any of the bases, just a few meat sacks lingering around in search of food. With a diesel generator and an armed force, we should be able to establish ourselves even more easily than we did in Fort Carson.

Jenny resists. She feels safer behind the military wall than on the road. I try to convince her that we can build a second Freetown. Both will be better off if we do. When she finally agrees to leave, she pleads for one more baby, one more toddler. She doesn't want to leave any children behind, but we can't take all of them with us. I try to convince her that they will be fine here.

Finally, exasperated with her, I answer, "We can take one more. That one." I point at her bulging belly. It's the end of September and Patience will be born in about two months. I smile to soften the blow. “You don’t remember to count her, but I do. I remember her, pink and pudgy. We’re solving a problem, Jenny. We don’t want to make the same mistake twice.” Still her eyes move over the nursery, over the children. “They’ll be fine. We aren’t taking that many sitters with us.” Fewer than I have hoped for. We’ll be understaffed as it is.

A plan in place, Heph and I volunteer for the next raid going east. Hopefully, we can find a base along the way, hijack the raiders, and clear out the base. Then most of us stay there while one or two drive back to get Jenny and the others willing to split off.

“Cassandra.”

I turn from the book I’m reading to look at John.

“You and Heph are on the next raid.”

It’s not a question. He plans all the raids. I nod in reply.

“You aren’t coming back.”

Again, it isn’t a question. I close my eyes and let out a slow breath. “Yes?”

"How many?" he asks.

"A little over a hundred."

He grunts. "You think you'll make it?"

I lift my eyes to his. "Do we have a choice? It's either try to live somewhere else or wait for you and the others to pick us off."

He frowns. "We aren't-"

"Bullshit!" I yell, desperate to let the anger and betrayal go. I keep it bottled when talking to Jenny and the others, but most of the boys coming with us have blown at one time or another. It's my turn. "You send us out at night! And how is it that every failure in the fence just happens to be right next to the nursery? Do you understand that we're all that is left of the human race?" That's probably an exaggeration. I think other countries have some survivors. It's unlikely many have the population we do. "We need to protect everyone," I remind him in a low growl. "If we can't do that here, we do it elsewhere."

He nods. "I'll come with you on the raid."

I blink in confusion. "What? You think we want some overlord coming with us?"

"No," he answers quickly. "I'm sure that's the last thing you want. But I'm a soldier, Cassy. I can help you secure another base. I can take you to one."

My scowl melts away. He's right of course, and I relax. "That would be great. Which base?"

"I'm thinking Fort Hood. I was stationed there for a little while."

Still fighting disbelief, I wonder, "Where is that?"

"Texas."

"Texas," I echo, mind spinning. "That should be good, a little warmer than here."

"Don't rub it in. I might jump ship with you."

I chuckle. "Thanks, John. Who else is on the raid?" We both know it's not a normal raid anymore.

"You tell me. Who do you want?"

Again, I blink in surprise. "Brian," I answer, "and Nick."

"I figured they'd follow you. A couple more?"

I name the five top guys in our separation sect.

"Sounds good. We leave tomorrow at dawn. Long way to go."

My eyes follow him as he walks back to the administration building. Did that really just happen? I hop up to tell Heph.

***

Heph's hand comes to rest on my hip. "The last of the ammunition is loaded. Ready?" John stayed with the others holding Fort Hood, Heph and I have returned to Freetown, Fort Carson, to pack up our separatists. A trio of buses waits at the gate. Jenny's with the children at the front. Older kids fill the next two. No one older than nineteen is coming with us. People come rushing up and others stick their heads through bus windows to say goodbye. It's taken Heph and me four days to get everyone rounded up and they are still lingering.

The munitions are just to protect us along the way. Fort Hood has its own stores that we'll be tapping. Also, Austin isn't far from the base and is relatively intact. As soon as we get the buses unloaded, Heph and Nick and I are planning a raid for food and other supplies. Starting over.

I take one last look at my home. I really don't know what's going to happen anymore. I don't know if we'll be safe, but I'm taking the people I care about most with me.

Grabbing Heph's hand, I climb the stairs of the bus and sling my rifle from my shoulder to between my feet, holding the barrel. We aren't likely to run into trouble on the road, but guards are posted throughout the bus anyway. The meat sacks won't have any idea how to stop us and the driver will run down any animals dumb enough to get in our way.

Once through the open gate, the bus turns south. A few of us look through the back to watch the gate close. It won't open for us again.

We stop to refuel twice, activating abandoned pumps, sometimes using our small generator. We have a larger one as well, just in case the ones on the base are damaged. Heph and I smuggled it onto one of the buses days earlier. Although we appreciate John's help, we're sure the council wouldn't authorize our taking it.

Our group is equally split between male and female. There are a few more males in the younger age bracket and a few more female teens, but the totals are even. Will we devolve the same way? Maybe, but I am pretty sure the maternal instincts of these ladies will rub off on everyone, making us all a little more civilized, separating us a little further from the monsters we fight. Something I'm not confident saying about Freetown.

"What are we going to call it?" Heph asks.

"What? What are we going to call what?"

"The base, where we stop, what are we going to call it?"

"Oh, uh, I dunno. I like Freetown."

"New Freetown?" Heph suggests with a smile.

"True Freetown," one of the ladies holding an infant suggests. The baby is nearing a year, probably not an infant anymore.

"Liberty!" someone else shouts.

“I like Liberty,” I say softly, not wanting to discourage more suggestions.

“Yeah, I like that,” Jenny agrees.

Heph nods as do many others. Fort Hood, a.k.a. Liberty.

We pull in for our third gas-up and I cover the doors as Heph and another boy lug the generator out of the bus and into the service station. Heph is back in a flash, plopping the hose into the tank. Two guys are at the back of the bus, watching in either direction.

I hear them first. “Guard up!” I shout, turning in the direction of the grunt. “Jenny, close the doors,” I yell over my shoulder into the yellow tin can. There is a creak behind me to let me know she heard. Tucking the butt of the shotgun into my shoulder, I wait for them.

The crunching of gravel and trash is the only sound for a while. They’ve stopped growling. I can’t decide if that’s good or bad. The first dirt-streaked face peers around the corner of the service station and I shoot it, right in the nose. The meat sack falls in a heap. Another is right behind it, and I dump the cartridge to load the second shot, taking aim again. The second goes down as fast as the first, but now I'm messing with my strap to load third and fourth shots. I wish for an automatic even though these high caliber guns are more efficient at stopping the monsters. Another gun fires behind me, taking down a third meat sack, but they keep coming, more than I've seen in one place for weeks.

They eventually feed on each other when the fresh meat runs out, limiting the number that are in any one group, but somehow, this group is made of at least thirty. We don't have enough ammo without going into the bus to reload. I wait for the last of the rifles behind me to fire before looking over my shoulder at Heph, still at the pump, cursing at the thing to go faster.

"Goodbye," I tell him and run straight at the group. I have no intention of letting them catch me, but I want enough of them to chase me that the rest have time to reload, regroup and maybe get the generator back on the bus.

Nails and teeth bite into my skin, but I pull away, tossing one body into another until I'm on the other side of the group and can hear them groaning and growling as they follow.

I don't know this town, I'm not even sure I saw the name when we came in, but I take the next right and then a left. I try to zigzag in a more-or-less straight diagonal from the bus, hoping to be able to find my way back. After five turns, I don't hear the chase anymore. I circle back to the bus, still running at my best speed, ignoring a stitch that's growing in my side.

Coming around the last corner to the service station, I stumble and nearly fall. The meat sacks are here, and they're feeding. The occasional shot rings out, but they are few and feeble. I dodge a blow by sheer reflex, grabbing the animal's limb and throwing it to the ground. I kick it in the face several times, hard, breaking nose and jaw, and finally windpipe. Then my attention is all back on the bus. I can see the little ones banging on the windows to get out while the sitters are all at the front, firing wildly with guns they only barely know how to shoot. I watch one get pulled out by her leg.

Heph, I think, wondering where he is, how he's fighting. I start to run toward the bus, but before I go three strides I'm blown backwards by an explosion. I cover my head as soft and hard pieces pelt me. What exploded? I peek out through my elbow to see the burning remains of a bus, blown out. The meat sacks immediately around it are all gone but there are still a few around me.

Pulling out a long knife from its holder on my belt, I set to work mutilating and finally killing my attackers. The grief and rage of what just happened fuel me and make me crueler than usual. I maim and break rather than kill. I scream my hurt, wanting to kill every last animal that took my second family from me. The babies. Jenny. Heph. As I move nearer the bus, I see his boots.

Mark comes out of the station with his gun up. "Cassy, inside," he calls, holding the door for me.

I hesitate but finally do as he asks, barricading the door behind us. “Who? I couldn’t see. Who?”

“It was Jenny,” he says, sounding as choked as I feel. “I think she was grabbing grenades.”

We hadn’t brought many grenades, but there were open fuel lines. “Jenny,” I whisper. “Patience!” I wail. Losing control, I start sweeping items from shelves, kicking coolers and freezers. I stop when I’m fairly certain I’ve broken my toe. “What do we do now?” I ask through sobs and the pounding on the half metal door.

“I was hoping you knew.” He crouches in front of me and I notice for the first time how pale he is. “Do you know what you look like?”

I shake my head.

“One of them. You’re covered in...”

He doesn’t have to finish. I pull off my shirt and use the inside of it wipe my face and arms, anything to not be like one of them. Mark is good and doesn’t stare, rather finding some crappy tourist tee for me to pull on. I’m stuck for the pants, and as I look down, I cringe to think what the rest of me looks like, what's probably in my hair.

"What do we do?" he asks me this time.

Taking a deep breath, I know the answer. "We keep going."

"But the bus."

"We'll hot wire something in town. The real problem is getting out of here without being eaten." I look around, hoping for something I can use. I come up empty.

"Here," he suggests, grabbing a handful of emergency flares. "They should blind them at least, right?"

"Yeah, they do hunt by smell."

Mark frowns and continues to look around. He grabs a big bottle of mouthwash.

"You're kidding, right?"

He up-ends the bottle over his arm.

"Meh, better than nothing," I reluctantly agree and grab my own bottle of Scope, pouring it into my hair. Maybe it will wash some of the shrapnel and gore out.

Dripping in minty goodness and armed with our rifles, we head to the back door. The sacks aren't waiting, but come at the sound. Mark and I are ready. He's shooting while I'm loading and vice versa. We keep going until our straps are empty. He's ashy when he looks at me. "Run out the front." Then he runs straight into the wall of flesh-eating animals.

Not quite believing my eyes or my ears, I turn and run to the front of the store. Most of them have left, but there are still several waiting for me. I try to make a break through them, swinging my shotgun like a bat. There's a weird red thing just past the mob.

I'm not even surprised when hot hands grab me and teeth bite into my neck.

CHAPTER EIGHT

I'M BLINDED by the bright summer sun, so different from the cloudy autumn day I left behind. The surf rushes in and soaks my legs while the breeze blows my hair across my face. I don't have to turn to see my parents to know it's July 10th, again. I lean against one of the boulders for a moment to think. What did I learn that can help me this time, the third time? I'm not going to kill the doctor, that's pointless, but I do need to get into his lab. Something there causes this and it's already there, the doctor has already done it, whatever it is. If I get into the lab, maybe I can figure that out.

But, since I already know it is done, I don't need to abandon my parents on the beach. I can go home with them and find a way into Manson tomorrow. Maybe they need summer staff. Not like I'd miss the job at the ice cream shop.

"Cassy? Aren't you getting wet?" my mother asks with a laugh.

"Well, I am in the water," I answer with a smile. I'm going to appreciate every moment I get to spend with my parents this time, not alienate them with strange behavior.

Heph. I wonder if I should try to contact him this time. It didn't end well for him last time, and he had a rough ride before we left. On the other hand, can I do this without him?

I walk further along the beach with my parents, enjoying the rest of the day before heading home. Everything is so placid, so peaceful, that I fall asleep in the van on the way home and Mom has to wake me. I try to remember ever sleeping so deeply. It was probably the first time, before I knew what was coming, what to expect. That fear will keep me on edge for the rest of time, unless I find a way to stop it.

It's late when we get home, but I pull up Manson's website, looking for internships or janitorial positions. I hit pay-dirt on the second. They're looking for cleaning staff, evenings and weekends. I mail in an application before hitting the hay. I'm not very tired, and toss for a while before turning my computer back on. With a smirk, I remember a way I can be in touch with Heph, one that won't have him wondering who I am or what I know. He'll just be wondering how he can kill me. Setting up an account as Seeressof2016 I log in and start searching for KnightRider.

***

I call up Manson the next day, checking that they've received my application. The HR lady seems surprised by the call, and impressed. She asks if I could come in for an interview that afternoon. Biting back a squeal at my luck, I run down the stairs to let Dad know I'm borrowing the old Taurus for a job interview. He's surprised as well.

"I thought you were working at the ice cream parlor?"

"Yeah, well, this looked more promising. It's more hours and better pay." Only barely, but he doesn't need to know that.

"Well, as long as it's enough to cover your costs. Driving to and from Albuquerque every day will get expensive."

"I'm sure. Thanks, Dad."

The only other call I have to make, I make in person — Mr. Brown deserves that much. He smiles as warmly as the last time, as the first time, when I enter the store.

"I have some news, Mr. Brown. I applied for a job in Albuquerque as well, and I have an interview today, so I won't be able to make my shift tonight. I'm really sorry for the short notice." I do my best sad-puppy face. He seems unaffected by it.

“I’m really sorry to hear that, Cassy. Do you know anyone who might take your place?”

I bite my lip for a second before sacrificing my friend. She turned on me so quickly the last time and didn’t survive either last time or the first, so it’s not as though she’ll have the job long.

“I think my friend, Julie, is looking for summer work. Let me call her.” Pulling my phone from my pocket, I hear it ring outside the door. I supposed it was about the time I ran into her outside the shop last time.

“Hey, Cass. Where are you? I thought we were making birthday plans.”

“Yeah, sorry about that. I have to bail on today. I have a job interview.”

“Interview? I thought you were working for Old-Man Brown.”

I take a deep breath. “I was, but I was sort of hoping you might take my shifts for me.”

There is silence on the other end of the line — a very bad sign. I don’t recall Julie ever being speechless.

"You thought I would like a job at the ice cream shop?"

"Yeah, you know, extra cash, lots of cute boys stopping by."

"Lots of bratty kids with pushy parents," she reminds me.

"Yeah, but they tip well." I'm stretching and I know it.

There is a loud sigh through the speaker. "Fine. I'm at the shop anyway." The bells on the door jingle as she walks in. "Oh," she says, disconnecting the call, "you're here, too."

The group of girls from the last time are with her again. They all seem to eye me strangely. I look down, wondering if I dressed poorly. Not that I can tell. This is a million times better than what I wore in Freetown.

"Have a good time in Cali?" Julie asks.

"Yeah, it was all right. Thanks for doing this, Julie. I kinda left Mr. Brown in the lurch."

"Hi, Mr. Brown," Julie greets him. "What was her shift?"

"Six to close, Tuesday through Friday."

"Friday night?" she whines.

Mr. Brown nods. "Yes, but we close at ten."

"Oh, well, that's okay then." I wonder why before remembering that most parties were barely underway by ten. My birthday was scheduled to start at nine. "I guess I'll see you tonight."

Mr. Brown nods. "I'll show you how to close up. And Cassy," he adds to me as we turn to leave. "Try not to do this to future employers. Burning bridges isn't good for your employment prospects."

I have to fight the hysterical urge to laugh. My future. There were no employers in my future, no pay, just running and surviving.

Julie doesn't take my arm this time, doesn't bubble with news.

"What was that about, Cassy? Why'd you drop your summer job on me?"

"I got another. I'm going to be working in Albuquerque."

Julie's face brightens a little. "Oh. Well, that's good. We're still having the party on Saturday, right? You aren't skipping your birthday?"

"I hope not. This job is weekends." Julie's eyes narrow in anger. I sidestep quick. "But I think it's weekend days, not nights."

"Good. Let's go work on the guest list. I think Amy Richardson isn't going to make it." She and the other girls start giggling before filling me in on the latest scoop on Amy Richardson. I realize that I still don't know who she is or why I would care about her spilling her lunch on Tracy Hudson's boyfriend. I nod and giggle and gasp in all the right places. I want to keep my waves small this time.

After lunch, I hop in the car and drive to my interview. It turns out to be little more than a formality. They've been looking for cleaning staff, but most people are freaked out about the biologic waste. I assure the lady in HR that I'm not easily grossed out, that I know the use of various chemicals and how not to mix them. She gives me a huge WHMIS handbook anyway, listing all the chemicals and substances I might come in contact with. The size of the book nearly grosses me out, but not the contents.

“How soon can I start?” I ask at the end.

“How soon would you like to start? I can get you a badge in time for the six o’clock shift.”

“Sounds good,” I answer with an eager smile. “I’ll just text my parents to let them know.”

“Really? Okay. Wait here and fill this out.” It’s a form for the company benefits plan. Wow, I could have health coverage, if there was an HMO left in two weeks. I fill out the form anyway; anything to get me access to Evans’ lab a little bit sooner.

An hour later, I have my badge. Two hours, I’m being introduced to Beryl, the grey-haired woman who supervises the night shift.

“If a door is locked, don’t open it. They don’t want you in there. Everywhere else, you clean around. If there’s something in the sink, you can wash it, but do not move anything into a sink or trash bin unless it’s on the floor.” She continues to shoot off instructions which the other staff ignore. Apparently, every new hire gets the same spiel.

"You got all that?" Beryl asks, hands on ample hips.

"Yep. Don't touch it unless it's on the floor."

"All right. I'm going to pair you with Jane for tonight. Follow her and do what she does. You'll fall into the routine."

I do; I shadow Jane through lab after lab, wiping surfaces with disinfectant, mopping floors, restocking plastic gloves. The job is monotonous, tedious, and perfect for letting me plan my next move. In Evans' lab, I can't help but go slowly over everything, hoping to find some hint of the virus.

I have little luck the first night. Vials and test tubes fill racks. Rabbits make scurrying sounds in their cage, echoing the rats in theirs. I can't thumb through notes or turn on computers with Jane along. She accompanies the next two nights, so the first lab workers are already running a fever by the time I am able to work alone and flip through pages at will.

The notes are mostly over my head. Kenny taught me a little, but nothing that would make sense of this. I make some notes. Maybe we can actually find a cure for it. It seemed impossible before, but maybe.

The rabbits have been injected. The rats were scheduled to be injected yesterday, but Dr. Evans didn't make it in due to illness. I jump up from my perch on a lab stool at the sudden screech filling the air. There is a pause and then another screech. I follow the sound to its source: the rabbit cage. One rabbit is attacking another, biting. Sickened, I put the notes back as they were and move onto the next lab.

At the end of the shift, I leave a note of resignation. I have all the information I need, I think. The rabbits are infected. According to the notes, they were the first mammals to encounter the virus, and like so many others would in the days to come, it turned them into flesh-eating monsters; small, furry, adorable monsters. I wish I'd never watched Monty Python with Dad.

That night, I post my anonymous warning. If you don't want to end up like the Manson employees, seal yourselves off. If you don't want to be hunted and eaten as animals, find somewhere secure to hide. I sign it Seeressof2016. Then I pack my bags and load the Taurus. Tomorrow night is my party, and I'm going to pretend that everything is normal, that my Mom and Dad are just sick, like everyone else's. I'm going to dance, drink, maybe have a smoke. I'm going to be as carefree as I was the first time. And when my parents come to eat my friends, I'll take as many as jump in the Taurus with me, and we will run.

***

Heph is heading up a group of other boys who have armed themselves and are keeping the swarms of meat sacks at bay when I meet him this time. I'm saddled with two of my more vapid friends. Their only virtue is that they can run fast.

"Please, will you protect us?" Olivia asks, practically hanging off Heph. I fight the urge to roll my eyes and only sigh.

"Do you have any extra arms? My parents weren't hunters," I explain.

"Huh? Oh, yeah, sure. We nearly emptied the outfitters." Heph passes me his rifle. "There, that shouldn't be too heavy for you."

Although I keep coming back in time, to a time before I had trained, I still seem to be strong enough to do all the things I did at the end of the first time. Guns are never too heavy, I don't tire quickly. It makes me wonder how much is physical and how much is simply expecting my body to be capable.

"Yeah, this is good. You want one Liv? Jessica?" I ask the girls. Both shake their heads.

"I don't know how to shoot a gun," Jessica whines.

"You should learn," Heph insists. "Best way to get a meat sack off your back is to shoot it in the head." One of his compatriots does just that, aiming for a man fifty yards away.

I turn back quickly while the girls continue to stare at the fallen corpse. "We should move."

Heph nods in agreement. "Too long in one place isn't good. We are holed up inside a warehouse. No windows, two exits, pretty easy to guard."

"Sounds perfect." I smile with relief. The girls and I haven't stopped for more than moments in the last two days.

"Follow me."

Heph turns to lead us and I hear Olivia behind me. "He's cute. Do you know him?"

"No," Jessica answers, "but I want to."

There were so few girls the first time, and the two of us were obviously connected in the second. I've never heard other girls take stock of Heph. I decide I don't like it. Lengthening my stride, I take a place beside him.

"How many in your posse?" I ask, looking at the boys surrounding us.

"Huh? Oh, six, I think. Assuming they're all still alive. Just you three in yours?"

"Yeah, and we aren't much of posse, unarmed and all."

He smiles and I instantly regret keeping my distance this time. "Well, that's not a problem anymore."

I chuckle and swing the gun a little. “Nope. Thanks again.” There is a soft squishing and I turn with the rifle in my hands, just as one of the girls screams. It’s my bullet that pierces the deranged woman’s head.

“Nice shot!” Heph cheers. “That your first kill?”

I think about that. I can’t really tell him that my kill count, cumulative, is near five hundred. Instead, I restrict my count to this time. “My second. I ran one over in the car before it crapped out on us.”

“That was so scary, Cassy. Why didn’t you go around him? I thought he was going to come right through the windshield.” Jessica hugs herself and one of the other boys put an arm around her shoulder.

I shake my head. “Getting to the car was scary. Running since the car quit has been scary. Driving over a breathing corpse? That’s just efficient.”

Heph laughs. “I like you. The car is toast?”

I sigh loudly and kick an empty drink cup down the equally empty street. "Yeah. It was a nice old Taurus, but she started to smoke, so we ditched it."

"Bummer," Heph says in agreement. "We could really use some trucks or vans, but most of the adults crashed them."

I nod. The fever and delusions could hit at almost any time. Dodging something that wasn't there could wrap your car around a tree that was. It was the same problem we had the first time.

"So, you're Cassy?" he asks.

"Seeress," I tell him, using the name he's more likely to recognize.

Heph remembers me. I can't help but smile when he does a second take at my nickname. "Seeressof2016?!" he shouts. The boys all cock rifles, expecting meat sacks to come pouring onto this street at the noise.

"Keep it down, boss," one tells him.

He softens his voice. "You posted the warnings?"

I nod.

"How did you know?"

I take a deep breath before answering. "I lived it."

His brow furrows as do my friends'. "What are you saying, Cassy?" Olivia asks.

"Why didn't you do more than post a single warning message?" Heph asks.

"I did." I don't explain. "Give me a little bit of time?"

He frowns, but doesn't argue. "We're nearly there." He knocks on the door of a warehouse and it opens for him. It isn't a special sequence because no meat sack would knock. There are three more boys inside, sitting around a small camp stove. The smell of cooking meat fills the air. The warehouse is large enough that any smoke has plenty of room to dissipate.

Although it's still summer, it is cooler in here without windows. All the light in the room comes from the stove and a few lamps near it.

Olivia and Jessica sit down quickly, obviously relieved. I continue to stand, keeping the rifle in my hands. Heph is watching me, although he pretends he's interested in the hot dogs.

"Aren't you going to eat, Cassy?" Liv asks.

"In a bit," I answer shortly, eyes going from one door to the other. A hand on my arm nearly makes me jump out of my skin and I barely stop short of firing the rifle at the ground.

"It is fairly safe here. They aren't going to sneak in," Heph reminds me. "You'll hear them come through the door."

He's right, of course, I'm just paranoid after being on the run for two days straight.

"Right. Do you have any water?" I ask, letting the rifle fall to my side.

"Plenty," he answers, pulling out a jug and bottle. Filling the bottle, he hands it to me. I notice it shake in my grip. I'm not scared, so I chalk it up to over-active nerves, one too many hours without sleep. "Sit down," he insists, keeping me just a bit away from the others.

I can hear Olivia and Jessica flirting with the boys but don't pay them any mind.

"Drink," Heph orders, tipping the bottle to my lips.

As soon as the liquid touches my tongue, I begin gulping. How long since I had more than a sip or splash of water between running? I can't recall before hitting the bottom of the bottle.

"Better?" Heph asks, his blue eyes full of worry. "Do you think you can eat something?"

The dogs smell a hundred times better now. "Oh yeah," I groan over a grumbling from my tummy. Heph chuckles but doesn't say anything else. We both turn to join the group. I think I recognize the guys, but after many faces, so many dead, I don't keep track of as many as I should. It wouldn't surprise me if these guys made up Heph's posse the first time.

Heph hands me a dog in a bun, wrapping my hands around it. I chuckle and pull it back.

"I'm not quite that bad," I tell him.

He smiles a little. "Good."

My friends continue to display their vapid natures. I watch Heph's eyes roll in my direction several times. I don't blame him; I can barely tolerate them. They are exactly the type of girls he hates, overly emotional.

At least they aren't trying to hit on Heph now that they've met some of his prettier posse. I don't think much of them. If they didn't survive long enough for me to remember their names, they can't be that great.

"So, Seeress," Heph says quietly. "Want to tell me why you didn't give us more warning?"

My dog is long gone, but Heph refilled my water and I take a drink. "Okay. I was afraid of saving too many people."

His brow furrows. "Too many?" he asks, slightly hoarse.

Other heads turn to us. All of his posse and Jessica are looking at me. Olivia is paying more attention to the boy with his arm around her shoulders than me.

"I've done this before," I tell them, "twice." No one seems to breathe, so I continue. "The first time, I didn't know what was happening. I was alone when I found you and you took me in." I glance at his friends but focus on Heph. "You taught me how to survive, how to fight back. I still died, but we lived for months before that."

"Months," Heph murmurs in disbelief.

I nod but return to my story. "When I died, rather than...dying," I say for lack of a better word, "I woke up on the beach before the outbreak."

"So, you knew this was coming?" Heph asks.

"Yes. I tried to stop it. When that didn't work, I tried to warn as many people as possible. We had The Lord of the Flies instead of a safe place to hide. I didn't want that to happen this time, so I kept my warning smaller, vaguer."

"You let more people die," Heph tells me.

Sighing, I nod. "Not everyone!" I argue. "You knew and prepared. I saved Liv and Jess this time." I look at my friends and think they aren't the sort of people I was trying to save. "I posted earlier warnings, too, telling people to isolate themselves, prevent infection."

Heph frowns and looks at his friends. "I don't remember a post like that, do you?"

They shake their heads.

“Well, there was one,” I snap exasperated.

“Okay,” Heph says slowly. “So, what are we supposed to do now?”

I look at the camp stove cooling in the middle of our circle. “We go to Freetown.”

“And you know where that is?” I nod. “Then I guess we need to find a car. For now, sleep, all three of you.” He looks at Liv, Jessica, and finally me. “We’ll keep guard.”

I nod and find another patch of floor to curl up.

“Do you think Cassy will bite my head off if I go for the leader?” Jessica asks Olivia. I pretend I can’t hear them.

“She didn’t seem very interested in any of them. I say go for it.”

Great, I won’t even have Heph this time around.

Chapter Nine

"Cassy?" Heph asks quietly. He's lying beside me, sharing some warmth on the cooling autumn night. My fears about my friends stealing him away were unfounded. Both found bigger and better things to chase in Freetown. I never left him, and he never stopped looking out for me.

"Yes, Heph?" I roll over so we're facing each other, my nose nearly touching his. Shifting the sleeping bag, I tuck a little further into it, seeking all the heat it offers.

"You know this is a suicide mission, right?"

I frown. “What do you mean? We’ve done this twenty times already. Go in, get the kids, get out.”

“We’ve never tried to get them out when they’ve locked themselves in. We’re going to be attacked before we open the door to their compound.”

“So, let’s send them a message first.”

“How? We can’t get in. You know, I have a feeling there aren’t kids on the other side of the wall. I think they have locked themselves in so they don’t get infected. You suggested that, remember?”

I’d nearly forgotten. It had been months since I posted my warning. “So, let’s leave a pile of corpses and a note.” I smile broadly, but he doesn’t share my humor. “Should we abort? Head home?” Leaving Freetown is always difficult.

Heph shakes his head. “No, if they are kids, we need to help them.”

“Do you want me to watch first?” Neither of us can sleep without knowing the other is watching, protecting.

“Actually, I was hoping you’d do something else for me.” He tips his head toward mine, kissing my lips. “I know I could have died anytime in the last three months, and there is something I want to do before going head first into danger again.”

My eyes widen when he kisses me again, working his way down my neck. Heph doesn’t usually initiate. Even the second time, when we were joined at the hip, I had indulged in the physical first. The first time, our friendship had evolved into something more, but we didn’t share more than kisses. This Heph has always been my partner, needing me to guard his back, never straying toward whatever we call this. A soft body? A girl? A friend with benefits? He has untucked my shirt and started unfastening my pants before I regain sense enough to answer him.

“Do you really think this is a good idea? I mean, what might sneak up on us while we’re . . .” I can’t even finish the sentence. How embarrassing.

"I don't care." His bravado seems forced. He does care, as do I. Neither of us wants to die. "How about we take turns?" he suggests. His hand continues moving over my skin under my clothes, making me squirm. Suddenly heat isn't a problem. In fact, the shared double bag is far too confining.

"I'm first?" I ask in a squeak, rolling away to lie on my back.

His lips are nipping my ear as he says. "Yes. I'll keep watching." His hand moves faster, further, and I clutch his upper arm as the heat in the bag intensifies.

My small moans gain volume until I have to clamp a hand over my mouth to keep them down. Heph's eyes twinkle in the starlight, enjoying whatever he's seeing in me. Finally, his hand stops, and I take a series of shuddering breaths, coming down from the high I was on.

That means it's my turn. My eyes are well adjusted to the dark around us and I listen carefully for any intruders. When I'm satisfied I have scouted the situation, I begin lifting Heph's shirt and press myself tight to his side. He kisses my neck and breaths heavily.

"God, you feel good, Cassy, like you fit right into me."

I know what he means. It's what made the first month this time so hard. There is a chunk of me missing when we aren't together, the chunk that is hot and hard and longing.

I try to tease him as he did me, touching and retreating, stroking and then shifting and kissing. He is practically quivering when I stop, thinking I've heard something. I sit up, head turning in the direction of the sound. A bird hops out of a tree, rustling leaves. I sigh in relief. Most mammals have gone cannibalistic, but birds and fish and other animals haven't. It's not a meat sack. We're still safe and we both need sleep. When I tell Heph that, he argues.

"Just a little more," he pleads. Already our touching has gone further than we've let it in Freetown, further than ever before. We feel moderately safe in Freetown. Here, in the open, this seems far more dangerous and at the same time, more thrilling.

Rather than argue, I lose myself in his arms, in the feel of his skin against mine, the heat surrounding us.

Freetown is full of couples. There aren't that many girls, so those there have found themselves pursued by the entire complement of males. I got lucky; Heph stands high enough that no one wants to risk stepping on his toes. So once he demonstrated any interest in me, the others all backed off. It doesn't hurt that I am quick enough with hand-to-hand combat that I can throw out any undesired attention. I've only had to do that once.

A few moments after what we're doing, what we've done, sinks in, I jump out of the bag and pull my clothes back on. Grabbing my rifle, I hike the perimeter in a quick walk. With a growing sense of relief, I return to our tiny camp to find Heph fast asleep.

Taking a seat beside the sleeping bag, I smooth his hair, running my fingers through it over and over, watching him sleep between furtive checks of our surroundings. He's so peaceful when he sleeps, entirely unlike when he's awake.

When my head nods too heavily, I shake his shoulder. "Heph, wake up."

"Mmm? Oh, my shift?" he asks. The rustling in the bag can only be him donning his pants.

"Please. I'm going to pass out soon."

He takes my rifle and holds the bag open as I crawl in. Then his kisses each of my eyes, neither of which will stay open. "I love you," he murmurs just as I slip out of consciousness, safe under Heph's watch.

I wake with the sun bright in my eyes. I can hear rustling, but it's brief and controlled. It comes just before the aroma of coffee.

"Up yet, sleepy head?" Heph teases.

"Yeah," I croak, taking the enamelware cup from him. The coffee is strong, bitter and almost gritty with grounds. I drink it anyway, needing the caffeine burst to push me through the next hurdle. "Any word from the cell?"

That's what we've taken to calling holed up groups. This one sent a message not long before the power went out.

"Nothing. Ready to do this?" he asks as I wolf down a cereal bar.

"Yes, ready." I stash the wrapper back in the box and pull my rifle out of the back of the pick-up. Following Heph, covering him, we make our way into Tulsa.

We have set up our camp on the outskirts of town, where we hoped to run into few meat sacks. They're more likely to stay where they have a steady food source, even when that is each other. Taking the highway that leads into town, we start looking for likely strongholds. I point out the police precinct, and Heph checks it out right away. One of the monsters is waiting inside, but I dispatch it before he gets his hand off the door handle.

"Shit, Cassy, you almost hit me that time."

"I did not," I complain. True, my target was only a few inches wide of his head, but I cleared it easily. “Besides, would you rather I hadn’t shot?”

“Never said that,” he rattles off quickly, probably thinking about what could have happened in the few seconds it took for me to move in the doorway. “But that pretty much rules out a cell in here.”

He’s right. The meat sack would have found and eaten any humans hiding in the building. Chances are he was an officer who got trapped when he couldn’t figure out how to open the door.

“Where next?” I ask, dividing my attention between the building interior and the street outside. There could be another meat sack trapped in the police hall.

Heph pulls the door shut, and I turn my attention solely to the street. I spy movement in the shadows between buildings across the street and fire, a guttural roar accompanying the shot.

“You are frighteningly good at that.”

Heat fills my cheeks at the complement. “Thank you. Which way?” I ask again, looking up and down the street.

“School?” Heph suggests, pointing to one we can barely see in the distance.

“Doesn’t seem very defendable.”

Heph nods his agreement but lifts his rifle and heads in that direction anyway. “Still, kids like familiar places.”

He’s right about that. Cells have been found in churches and schools before. Windows are usually the biggest hazard. As we near the brick building, however, we can see that the windows are boarded up and the entire structure looks a little unstable. This time, I take the handle while Heph covers me.

The door is meant to open out, but I can only pull it a few inches before something catches and prevents further movement.

“What is it?” Heph asks when I don’t open the door.

“Pay-dirt,” I answer, peeking into the sliver of an opening. They have locked themselves in, but we can work around. Also, it's proof the ones hiding aren't meat sacks. Someone has tied the push handle on this door to the one next to it. Neither will open. Someone with a brain is waiting on the other side. Pulling my pocket knife, I slide it through the opening and saw at the rope.

With a snap, my knife drops and I almost lose my grip on it. The door falls shut, but when I grab the handle, it opens outward easily.

Heph continues to cover me, even though it seems impossible for a meat sack to have gotten in. There is a scurrying as the door closes behind me and two heads peek around a corner.

"We're okay," I tell the children. "We're not like them." Speaking is the fastest way to prove you aren't infected.

"Who are you?" the girl of the pair asks. She steps around the corner so Heph and I can see her clearly. Her coveralls are brown with ground in dirt and some blood. They're also torn in some places. Heph has his gun pointed at her.

“Put that down,” I hiss at him. “Or point it that way.” I point to the doors. He latches onto that idea and takes a position with his back to a wall. “I’m Cassandra and this is Heph. We’ve come to help if we can. How many are you?”

The boy is wearing clothes at least as dirty and ratty as the girl’s. Neither appears to be more than ten or eleven. “There are ten of us. Where did you come from?”

Neither the boy nor the girl can take their eyes off us. “We came from a place where there are no zombies. We have walls and a fence that keep them out. We bring in supplies from places outside, but it’s safe inside. We call it Freetown.”

The girl covers her mouth and nose, eyes tearing up.

“You have food in Freetown?” the boy asks.

“Yes, and more clothes. Lots of weapons,” I add, cocking my head toward Heph and his rifle.

“Come with us,” the boy says, turning the way he came. The girl falls in on my other side.

Heph doesn't move. "I'll guard the door until you come back. No sense locking it if we're leaving right away."

I nod in agreement and take the girl's hand. "What's your name?" I ask, remembering the techniques Jenny has taught me for keeping people calm.

"Bella," she answers, rubbing at the dirt on her face. Tears have made clear tracks on her cheeks. "We thought we'd never get out."

"Some of us go out, Bella," the boy says with derision. "How else would we have anything to eat?"

"Do you go on raids?" I ask him.

"No, I'm too little."

I don't answer that. He wouldn't be on raids from Freetown, either. Not for another year or two, anyway. The boy, his back is up a bit too much for me to try asking for his name, opens a heavy door labeled "Boiler Room." Bella pulls a little on my hand, advancing.

The room is dark. There aren't even barricaded windows here. It is also hot.

“What did you find?” a female voice asks.

“People,” the boy answers. “This girl and her boyfriend say they come from Freetown. They say it’s safe there.”

A teenaged girl, almost as big around as Jenny, moves to greet me. “Really?! Welcome. How far away is your Freetown? Can you take all of us?” She rubs her belly as she eyes me carefully.

“We have a pickup truck, so we should be able to fit all of you in the box. There are ten of you?”

The pregnant girl nods. “That’s right. Me, Peter,” she nods to the boy, “Bella, the twins Jackie and Jean, Matthew.” A boy comes to stand behind the girl, hands on her shoulders. I start to make my way through the boiler room to where a group of kids sit around a cloth on the floor, littered with playing cards. “Curtis, Brent, and David — they’re upstairs on guard. Joshua is asleep. He had guard last night.” She looks over her shoulder to a mat on the floor.

“I’m Cassy, Seeress.” I extend my hand, but no one takes it.

"You're the Seeress?" Matthew asks.

"You saw them coming?" Bella asks, her mouth hanging open.

"Yes, I wasn't able to stop them; only warn people."

The twin girls stand up from their game of cards. "You saved our lives," one says, wrapping her arms around my waist.

Instead of buoyed by the affection, I wonder how many more I could have saved by spreading the word farther, through more people. I wonder if I'll be able to stop the outbreak next time. I wonder if there will be a next time. Last time, the second time, I saved many more people, only to lose them when Freetown became overcrowded. Should I have done that this time as well, only started several Freetowns rather than one?

It is too late for what if. I don't know for certain that I'll get another chance. Maybe this time, when I die, it'll be for real.

"Are you okay?" the pregnant girl asks.

"Yeah. I didn't catch your name."

"Mary."

"Did your doctor give you a due date before . . ." I swing my arm in a circle.

"No. I only suspected I was pregnant a couple months ago. I got big fast."

'"There's another expecting mother in Freetown. She must be at least as far along as you."

Mary's smile broadens. "I'm not the only one who found the worst possible time to get knocked up?"

I laugh with her. "No. And we're pretty sure we have a few 'oopsies' in Freetown as well."

"Joshua," Bella says, crouching next to the young man on the mat. "We need you to wake up, Joshua."

He flinches and jumps up. It's the way I often respond when I wake up, flailing.

"It's okay, Josh," Mary soothes him. "Seeress is here. She's taking us somewhere safe."

Joshua's eyes narrow on me as he gets to his feet. "You are the Seeress?" he asks.

"Yes. I posted the warning. I'm also a resident of Freetown, where other survivors have built a home."

"How did you get in here?"

"Well, I'm not a zombie, so I'm smart enough to be able to cut a rope."

We're interrupted by three boys crashing through the door.

"There's a guy with a rifle out there."

"Why are the doors unlocked?"

"Who is she?"

Mary shakes her head. "Everyone settle down. Especially you, Josh. Cassy has come from somewhere with enough people that they don't only risk going out for supplies, they come looking for kids like us. We're going back with her. Whoever they are, they're in a better position than us."

Jackie and Jean both nod emphatically, although Matthew seems less sure than before and Joshua is entirely unconvinced.

"Look, you can stay if you want to, but our truck leaves in half an hour. We're just outside town to the north." I don't try to convince them further. If they really want to make a go on their own, I wish them luck. I wish more had tried that last time.

I leave the boiler room and make my way back to Heph. He still has his rifle pointed at the door.

"Relax, soldier," I tell him. "You're going to give yourself a wicked neck cramp."

"Too late," he says, working his head from side to side. "Where are they?"

"Coming." I pull him from the wall enough to stand behind him and rub his shoulders. "They seemed a little uncertain of me."

Heph snorts. "If they don't trust you, I would have scared them right off."

I chuckle. "Probably. I told them we're leaving in thirty minutes, with or without them."

Heph nods and then tucks his chin further, bowing his head while I work on his neck.

A scraping and grinding brings both our heads up to focus on the door. Heph puts the rifle to his shoulder even as I'm swinging mine into place.

We both open fire as one meat sack manages to yank a door half-open.

There is shuffling down the hall, but I'm already kicking at the door while Heph picks off heads. His rifle is joined by two more as two of the boys from the boiler room open fire as well.

I look out the door and shake my head. "Cut it!" I grab the handle and pull back on it, fighting the strong arms of a full-grown man. "There are too many. We can't get out this way, not right now."

Heph fires twice more before helping me haul the door shut. One of the boys reties the rope.

"It's too short. It won't hold."

"Where did they all come from? I thought there were only a fifty or so left in the city." Matthew is in the stairwell, apparently looking out through gaps in the second story. "There are hundreds out there."

"They like fresh meat," I say sadly. "They followed us." I look down for a moment and notice a scuff mark on the tile floor. "Are the labs stocked at all?"

Heph grins. “Bomb.”

I nod. “Bomb.”

“I think we’ve used everything,” Matthew warns. “But you can take a look.”

Heph trots up the stairs while I stand point at the door. It’s rattling as the sacks shake it.

“Mary, go back to the boiler room. Take Bella and the twins with you. Just in case.”

Mary nods and the girls don’t argue when she herds them away.

“Are only the two of you armed?”

“I can be in a second,” the third boy says and runs past Mary on his way back to the boiler room.

“Give me that,” Joshua says, pulling the gun from one of the younger boys.

“But...“

“Find another.”

I already dislike Joshua. “Here,” I say, passing my best weapon to the younger boy. “I’ll use these.” Reaching behind me, I tug twin blades free of their scabbards.

"You aren't seriously going to fight hand-to-hand," Joshua scoffs.

"This is what I have. If you can't keep them back with those, then yes, I plan to use these." I strike a ready stance that Heph drilled into me the first time. We still practice together regularly. As I half expect, the shots behind me start to die off and meat sacks climb over their own corpses through the doorway.

Turning to the side, my blade moves with me, nearly taking the head right off the first animal. It falls back, hanging by the strip of skin and flesh on the back of its neck. Blood gushes from the body, spraying me, but I turn the other direction, bringing my other knife into play and using the momentum to thrust the headless creature into his fellow. I strike at one more neck before a gunshot takes the head completely.

Backing up, I resume my ready stance. They boys have all reloaded, but that round of ammo will run out as well. It does and I surge in, trying to push my way out the door and into them. I need to see how many there are, how we can get out of this.

There are still too many crowding the stairs and walk leading to the school.

"Cass! Get back!" I hear from above and obey. It's Heph's voice, and before I'm back inside, liquid is splashing down on the hoard, making them scream and howl.

Boots and shoes thunder on the stairs as Heph and Matthew return. "That's all we have. How'd it do?"

"Great," I say with a wide grin, pushing over the bodies again into the blinded and disrupted group. My knives find throat after throat even as gunfire opens nearby. Heph's at my back with a pair of Glocks. He isn't wearing his rifle, but I hear heavier shots from the doorway. Someone in there has it.

"Three o'clock," I suggest, nudging him slightly with my hips to indicate the direction I think we should move.

"Three," he agrees and I feel his heat leave my back. I take careful, sliding steps backward, moving the pair of us out of the sight of the door and making their targets that much easier to hit. Heph and I are mowing down the injured, but untouched zombies are pushing their way up the stairs, hungry for us.

We move together through the crowd, putting blades and bullets ahead of our progress. The fight gets bloodier, hotter when the uninjured push up the stairs.

"Retreat?" I suggest, looking back to the door.

"Not sure. It's pretty blocked."

He's right, the pile in the doorway is almost unpassable. Thankfully, we're putting a dent in their numbers. Between panting breaths I manage to ask, "What did you hit them with?"

Heph snorts while sliding a clip into his gun. "Bleach. The cleaning closet was untouched."

I can't help but chuckle even though it means some of the blood gushing from my latest victim gets in my mouth. I'm covered in it now and Heph is only marginally cleaner.

"Down," he says, jumping off the side of the stairway, hopping the rail.

I set one blade on the metal rod, bracing my weight in my wrist as I swing over the edge. It only takes moments for the sacks to come for us.

"Six hundred," I murmur as I take another head.

"No way! I only have two hundred tops and I know I've killed more than you."

"This time," I say with a smirk. The numbers are dwindling all the time. I'm a little surprised when the heavy fire from the rifles returns. Looking up, I see Joshua and one of the other boys standing at the railing, shooting down into the crowd. At the same time, the surge around us starts to shift, some going for the stairs again.

"Inside!" Heph shouts up to them. "Pick them off from upstairs." As he finishes the word, the meat sack in front of him loses its head to a bullet.

"Mary's already up there with Matthew," Joshua shouts. However, the deafening roar from the mob is lessening, just like their population. We're getting to the last of them. In fact, two turn and run, something I've only seen once or twice before. Heph and Joshua each hit one, taking them down.

I lean against the concrete stairs, panting. “Is that it?”

“Yeah, but there might be more hiding somewhere,” Heph reminds me and holsters his guns. “We should make our way to the truck now.”

“Sure,” Joshua agrees quickly. “We just need to clear the door enough for the girls to get out.” His smirk is friendlier than it seemed before.

“You mean Mary,” Heph says with a chuckle.

“Yeah. She’s not very agile right now.” They share another laugh, but I’m already shifting bodies, rolling a couple down. I see Mary, Bella, and Matthew through the gap. The other boys and the twins have climbed out over the pile and are standing with Heph and Joshua. I reach out to Mary, helping her over the obstacle. Matt supports her from the other side.

“You can make it,” I assure her. “Just crouch through the opening and you can stand up on this side.” I’m feeling less urgent by the minute. The pile of meat sacks is so high, I wonder if there are any left in the city.

Mary's nose wrinkles at the bodies beneath her, the blood smudging her oversized dress, but she makes it out. The rest are quick to follow, having less trouble with the uneven surface of the stack.

I want nothing more than to take a long shower and a long nap. The former I won't get until we return to Freetown. The latter I might manage in the box of the truck once we're in motion.

"You were beautiful back there," Heph whispers in my ear, "a real angel of destruction."

I snort. "I felt like an idiot savant. Why didn't I pack pistols?" I tap one of his holsters.

"Because you like to show off?"

I narrow my eyes but don't reply.

"I can't believe you did that," Joshua murmurs from behind me. "You were amazing. How did you not fall when they bit you?"

"Bit me?" I notice for the first time a burning in my arm. I see fresh blood dampening my sleeve. "Oh. I guess it only scratched. I didn't even notice."

Mary surges forward and starts pushing back my sleeve.

"Ow!" I shout, shoving her away. "It's not that bad, and that hurts. Just leave it alone 'til we get to the truck, okay?"

"Won't you become infected?" she asks.

I chuckle. "We're already infected, all of us. We're also immune. So no, I won't become infected."

"The bite will," Heph reminds me. "Those sacks of flesh still carry bacteria and other viruses."

"I'll clean it when we're on the road, okay?" I tell both Heph and Mary. "Promise. Right now, I want to be on our way back to Freetown."

"Deal," Heph says with a bark of a laugh. "I'll feel better once we're off.

When we arrive at the truck, I push Mary and Bella toward the cab. "You are too little for the box," I tell Bella, "and we don't want you or the baby getting sick. Hop in." I climb into the back, but Heph stops me. "Why don't you drive?"

"Because I'm dead on my feet. Wake me when we get there," I jest, pulling myself over the tailgate with the boys and twins.

"Here, Cassy, you can sleep on my shoulder," Jean offers and I can't help but smile. I sit next to her and tuck my head into the curve of her neck. She's only a little older than Bella, maybe thirteen, but she has this mothering thing down already. Not for the first time, I think about how I lack all those instincts. I've gotten tips from Jenny, I've tried to make myself more approachable, be more encouraging, and less sarcastic and abrasive. Any child I have will be sick of me before a month or two living with me. I'm still not sure why Heph and I are able to get along as well as we do. We are twice as harsh with each other most of the time.

I'm nodding off when a jolt of pain in my arm brings me up. "Ow!" I shout again, punching out at the same time.

"Dammit," Joshua cusses, though it is muffled as he's holding his nose in both hands. "I was just trying to clean it."

I groan and lean back into Jean, who is grinning like she's just seen the best thing ever. "Sorry. Be careful waking me."

"I will," Joshua adds sullenly, then he starts pulling my sweater up.

"What do you think you're doing?" My voice is cold and flat.

"I have to expose the bite to clean it."

I roll my eyes tiredly and reach back to free one of my knives. Then, sitting up a little, I slice away the stitches at shoulder. Dropping the knife, I pull down on my sleeve, tearing it free. The steel of my knife rattles as it bounces very quickly in the box.

Joshua picks the knife up.

"Thank you. That noise was annoying." I rub my temple, trying to take away the slight headache that's growing there.

"No problem," Joshua tells me, sheathing the blade again. Then he pours clear liquid over my bicep and I lunge at him again. He's ready this time, and I miss completely.

"What was that?"

"Vodka," he tells me. "We actually had a pretty good stash of alcohol, not that we used it much.

I chuckle. "Good thing Heph didn't know. He'd have burned down the school."

"He doesn't like schools?" Jackie asked.

I shake my head very slightly, still resting on Jean. "Not that." I yawn widely. "He just likes fire. Stupid pyro."

It's one of the less consistent things about Heph. The first time, we'd escaped the fires of Gallup together and he'd used the blazes as a strategy for escape. Last time, he never started a single fire. This time, we'd stayed in Gallup until it burned, again, and although he wasn't as bad as I made it sound, he did occasionally like to set fire to a dwelling that the zombies thought was inhabited.

"Well, we only brought a couple bottles with us, so hopefully he doesn't get any ideas."

I yawn again. “Yeah, I doubt he will.”

Jean strokes my hair. “Go on and sleep, Cassy, and thank you.”

“Thank you.”

“Thank you.” The last one is from Joshua. He sounds sincere.

Chapter Ten

"JENNY, HOW did you know you were pregnant?"

I've missed two periods in a row, but don't feel any different from a few months ago. Shouldn't I feel pregnant?

"I took a test. Why? Did you and Heph?" She doesn't have to finish the sentence. I'm beet red and she has her answer.

"Well! We have a few. The boys who raided the pharmacy probably didn't mean to swipe those with all the pain killers and condoms, but lucky for us, they did."

I'm not the first girl in Freetown to think she was pregnant. Only two actually were, but a girl came to the supply rooms for a test every couple of weeks.

"We haven't run out yet?"

"No. They swept the whole shelf, so we have lots of different brands." Jenny is grinning as she rubs her belly. Patience is due in a couple of days. I haven't told Jenny which day. I've tried to keep my information to myself as much as possible this time. "Ugh, would you just come already?" she whines to her baby as she bends to retrieve a white box from one of the lowest shelves. "Here you go. Use it first thing in the morning." She hands the box to me and it shakes in my grasp.

"Relax!" Jenny encourages. "Even if you are pregnant, the baby isn't coming for months."

"I can't be a Mom!" I cover my face and run from the supply room. Jenny follows, but in her condition, she has no hope of keeping up. I burst into Kenny's lab. Just as they did the first time, he and Jenny survive the outbreak and find

Freetown. His lab is actually one of the old tank bays, but the tank is currently out searching for more survivors.

"Did you learn how to do an abortion?" I blurt.

"What?" he drops the glassware he's holding and it shatters on the table. "What?" he cries again, still not paying any mind to the mess.

"I-I can't be pregnant," I try to explain.

"Cassandra?" He finally turns to face me, his green eyes full of shock. "You of all people know why I wouldn't help you abort, even if I did know how."

I sigh loudly. He has told me, not just this time, but every time. We need more people, more genetic diversity. We need each and every one if we're going to prevent the extinction of the human race as we knew it.

I know that, rationally. Irrationally, I'm crapping my pants. "I can't. I don't know how to be a mom."

Ken's shocked and somewhat angry expressions soften. "Oh, is that all?"

"All? That's everything! Once I'm a mother, I'll be a mother forever. It's not some quick, one-time job or task. It's for life!"

Kenny turns back to his table, allowing me to only see his profile. His red hair is shaggy and slightly curly. He has a red shadow on his jaw as well. He frowns at the mess. "I'm glad this was a replication," he mutters before finding cloths and starting to mop liquid and glass into a metal pail. "Cassy." He doesn't turn back to me, focusing on his table. "You aren't going to be the only one looking after your baby. You aren't the only one having a baby. There will be other girls who will happily look after your child, just as they are looking after the littlest survivors. You can't think Jenny would turn her back on a baby of yours."

"No," I admit, sheepishly. He's right. Jenny would take my baby as her own if I asked her. She might volunteer for the job when she sees what a piss-poor mother I make. "Hell, I might not even be pregnant. I haven't taken a test yet."

"There you go," Kenny says in agreement. "Nothing to worry about."

"I'm sorry I startled you." I scuff the toe of one combat boot on the floor. There was a surprising supply of women's sizes on the base.

"Don't worry about it. Like I said, just replicating results."

"What sorts of results?" I ask, approaching the table.

"Well, I've been trying to figure out what makes us immune, right?"

I nod.

"In order to block the virus so completely, I presume the antibody is in our blood. I've been isolating them, trying to figure out which one stops the change."

"But how can you tell? None of us change."

He points to a series of terrariums with a few hundred brown field mice inside. A pressurized air canister, which I was sure I saw with the ammunition a few weeks ago, is hooked up to it.

"Where'd you find them?" I ask, tapping the glass although most of the mice are asleep.

"In the storeroom," Ken answers. "I popped them in there as soon as I could and sealed it off. A few were infected, but since I isolated them, the rest have been fine." I examine the series of glass walls he uses to break the cage up.

"Wow. Nice set up. Think we could have kept any adults in cages like this?"

Ken shakes his head. "I don't think they'd stay inside, do you?"

I nod but look at the terrariums again. If I have to go through this another time, I might just set up an isolation shelter like this. "How long does the virus live without a host?" I ask.

"Less than twelve hours, more than eight." Ken's answer is evasive.

"You've found something?" If he's replicating results he must have found something worth examining.

"Yes. It's not a true antibody. It's actually a hormone; growth hormone, oddly enough."

There's a knock behind us and I turn to see Heph. "Cass? Can I talk to you a minute?"

"Sure, Heph. Thanks, Kenny."

"Anytime. Don't stress out, okay?"

"I won't."

"Is it true?" Heph asks, looking me over. "Are you . . .?"

I hold up the box under his nose. "I don't know yet. That's what this is for."

"Oh, but you think you are?"

"I think I might be."

"I'm sorry, Cassy. I never meant to—"

I laugh. "You better not finish that sentence. I'm pretty sure you meant to. Otherwise, I'll be offended and have to kick your ass."

"Of course, I meant that part! I love you, Cassandra."

I back up a little. He's told me this a few times, but it sounds wrong now. "You're not thinking you owe me something, I hope."

"Well, yeah. I have to help."

I chuckle a little and then giggle. "Heph, you'd be a worse parent than me, and that's saying something!"

"What's that supposed to mean?" He puffs up his chest and I realize I've hurt his feelings.

"I mean what Ken just told me. We aren't going to have this kid by ourselves. That's if I am pregnant, which we don't know."

Heph doesn't answer, just stares blankly.

"How many orphans are there? Who raises them? Don't you think any new babies would be cared for in the same way?"

"Oh, yeah, I guess so." He rubs the little stubble he's managed to collect on his chin. "Huh, guess it's not so bad then."

I nod. "Not now anyway. I might be cursing your name when I get to Jenny's size."

Heph's eyes widen and he stares at my midriff.

I shove him. "Knock it off. We'll find out tomorrow."

He is patrolling the perimeter at noon, so he can't see my hand shaking as I open the box and read the directions.

"I just pee on the stick?" I murmur aloud, surprised how simple the test is. I thought I'd have to draw blood or something. Carrying the device with me, I make my way out to the girls' latrine. A couple of the girls notice what is in my hand.

"Good luck," they all say, squeezing my arm or shoulder. I don't know if that means they hope it's positive or negative, but at just that moment I'm not so sure myself. A baby, can I really have a baby? Well, apparently I am physically capable or I wouldn't be holding this test.

I hold my breath as I walk back into the barracks, falling onto my bunk with a thump. It will be another three minutes until I can trust the result in the little window.

"Cassy, have you seen—"

Mary is cut off as I jump straight up and pull one of the knives from my back, sending the test sailing across the floor. It stops at her feet where she can't see it for the protrusion that is her own baby. She saw it slide and squats to pick it up.

"You're having a baby?" she asks, looking at the test.

"I am?" My voice shakes. "Really?"

Mary nods and comes closer to put her arms around me. "It's scary, I know." Her voice wavers a little as well. “You don’t believe you can do it. You wonder if there isn’t some way out. Then you think that you can’t let anything happen to change it. It’s confusing, frightening, and frustrating. Whose is it? Heph?”

I nod, my lips pressed tight together. “He isn’t ready either.”

“Neither am I and I’m a lot closer than you are.”

“Yeah, but you’re good with kids. Look at Bella, Jean, and Jackie.” The girls had been remarkably well adjusted for having spent two months locked in a school boiler room.

“They aren’t babies. I can handle kids; they can tell me what they want. But, a baby?”

I start shaking again.

“Where is Heph?” Mary asks, rising from where we sit on my bunk.

“Umm, on patrol.” The words are whispered, slurred, but she makes them out.

“I’ll get him for you. Don’t worry, Cass. You’ll do at least as well as I have so far.”

I don't believe her but nod to get her to leave. I'm still sitting there when Heph comes in. Looking up, I meet his eyes. If I'm as pale as he is, it's a wonder I'm still conscious.

"She told you?"

He nods. "How do you feel?" He sits beside me and takes my hands.

"Scared shitless." Taking a second, I try to get a handle on what I am feeling. "I think I'm more scared than I have been since the first time. Every time I've faced a meat sack I've had the sense that I can do this, I can do something about this. I don't have that now. I don't know how to do this, or even if I can." I don't realize I'm shaking until he puts his arms around me. Then I'm crying. He isn't, of course. Heph never cries. Even when he tells me he had to kill his parents to escape the house—that's happened twice now—he doesn't cry.

"It's okay, Cassy. You can do this. You are every bit as strong and capable as Jenny, or Mary, or any of the new ones." There are two girls that we know are pregnant and not showing. Now there are three.

"I don't think I can," I half-wail. "I'm just some dumb kid who can't even stop this virus from ruining the world."

Heph shakes me roughly, holding me out from himself. "You are not dumb. You aren't just some kid. You are the Seeress. You have helped us make this place."

I shake my head. "I did that last time. I got here first, started gathering people right away." I sniffle. "It didn't work. There were too many and the oldest started weeding the rest of us out. It was awful." I'm still blubbering a little. "We left, and then we died."

"You never told me that."

I wipe at my cheeks. "I know. I didn't want to explain why I didn't do that this time. I didn't want anyone to know I could have saved more." I'm less scared than ashamed now and flop into my pillow face down, crushing my glasses before pushing them roughly off my head.

I hear a soft click that can only be Heph putting them on my foot locker. “Cassy. I’m here for you, babe, but I can’t do this for you. I know you can do it.”

He leaves. He hates crying women. I know that and it makes me weep harder. I’m turning into his mother, or his sister. He’ll leave me like he left them.

“Cassandra?”

I sit up when I recognize the voice. “Yes? What is it, Jenny?”

“I heard. If you need someone to talk to . . .”

She’s offered the same to the other girls, I already know.

“Your baby, she’s going to be born in the next week.” I’ve never been that specific before. I’ve always worried that knowing might change things; that she might endure some stress she didn’t the first time and go into labor early, or not have the crisis she did the first time and take longer to go into labor. Now that I’m pregnant too, those details seem stupid and small.

“She?”

Did I forget to tell her it is a girl this time? I can't have. I always think of the fetus as Patience. She always is Patience. She was conceived before July 10, before the date I have cycled back to twice.

"Yes, she. She'll be healthy and beautiful, and you will be an excellent mother. Nothing like me," I mutter. The tears don't come back, and I'm less scared than before. I remember Jenny giving birth the first time. I remember how brave she was, how she endured the pain because Kenny didn't want to give her more than codeine. I can do that. I'm not afraid of pain. I'm afraid of responsibility. I'm afraid of having a baby that will rely on me for everything. It's starting to sink in that I don't need to be scared by that; my baby will rely on all of us. Everyone has been relying on me to find a way out of this. That has to be at least as bad as a baby, right?

"You're looking better already," Jenny muses, stroking my hair back. I lean my head on her bony shoulder, my nose in her yellow hair. "Next week? I don't know that I'm ready," she says with a quick giggle. "On the other hand, I'm ready for all this extra weight to go away, to be able to sleep on my stomach again. Enjoy it while it last, little momma."

I chuckle at that, straightening up. "Little Momma. I think I'm an inch or two taller than you."

She shakes her finger at me. "Don't you be talking back."

"Yes, ma'am," I answer cheekily. Then I hug her tight. "Thank you."

"Anytime, Cassy. I really do understand. I was practically comatose for the first month after I found out."

"You know, I don't think you ever told me who the father is." I remember the topic coming up last time, but we ended up talking about someone else.

Jenny stiffens slightly. "He isn't. He doesn't exist anymore."

I nod in understanding. Either he was older than her and infected, or immune and killed. Either way, she doesn't have to relive it. "But you have all of us for fathers now." After a moment, I add, "Heph's got it easy! I want to be the Dad."

Jenny laughs loudly. "Yes, he does. You'll be a fine Mom, Cassy. You have lots of time to prepare for it."

"Right." I pass a hand over my belly anyway, expecting something to be different when nothing can be, yet.

Jenny kisses my cheek before she leaves and I'm just washing my face at a washbasin when Heph enters again. I trot over to him and hug him. "I'm sorry I lost it earlier."

"It's okay. It's a lot to deal with. I'm glad you're doing better now."

I smile and stiffen a little when he kisses me. I look around quick to make sure we're alone.

"It occurs to me," he says, running his fingers over my ribs and lifting the hem of my shirt, "that because you are pregnant, you can't get pregnant."

I can't help it; I laugh over his kisses. "You think that's romantic?"

"No, I think life's too short, and you're wearing too many clothes. Jenny's guarding the door for us. We have twenty minutes."

That information takes a second to process, but once it has I push him onto the bed, not wanting to waste a single minute of the twenty.

***

Sitting beside Jenny, I watch the littlest ones sleep. Asleep, they all look angelic, though I've seen the beautiful devils they turn into when awake. I do not envy Jenny or any of the other sitters. Patrolling and raiding both seem less onerous after watching the sitters and the littlest ones for a while. I would never have the patience.

Patience. She should come today. Jenny, sitting beside me, doesn't seem to be going into labor.

"Excuse me," she says for the third time in an hour. I wonder if her bathroom routine will ever be normal again.

"I'll come with you this time." Looping my elbow through hers, I lend her support on the slippery walks and grounds.

"Thanks," Jenny says, just before she slips. "Whoa!" she cries out, clutching at me. Planting my feet, I brace against her weight, holding both of us steady.

Jenny takes a moment upon righting herself to hold her belly. "Oh," she groans, "oh no."

My eyes widen as the inside of Jenny's XXL sweatpants become wet.

"It is today!" I grip her elbows in both my hands and turn her toward the infirmary. "Let's get you back inside."

She lets me lead her through the halls, occasionally squeezing my arm.

"Contractions?" I ask.

"I suppose." She sounds confused. "I thought I was just constipated." That's muttered and I'm not sure I heard it correctly. "There's another one."

"Let's get you to Kenny."

In the infirmary, a few girls and boys are listening to Kenny and writing in notebooks.

“Sorry to interrupt, but I have a patient.” I grin as I pull Jenny through the door with me.

“Labor?” Kenny asks. “She’s really in labor?” Blood drains from Kenny’s face.

“Relax.” I tell him as Jenny is swarmed by the students who help her up onto the exam bench. “I know you haven’t done this before, but I’ve seen you do it. The baby is fine, Jenny is fine. You won’t have any problems.

“You’ve seen it?” he asks. “You were there?”

I shake my head. “Not all of it, but you did it, and when I asked, Jenny said there weren’t any problems. So, relax. Remember what you’ve learned.”

He nods, but is still frighteningly pale. It makes the freckles on his nose starker, red-brown against white instead of pink.

“Maybe you should sit down for a minute,” I suggest. “You look like you’re going to faint.”

The kids are helping Jenny remove her pants and giving her a robe instead. They all seem excited, not nervous like Jenny or Kenny. After flopping into a chair and putting his head in his hands, Ken's color returns. In that time the students have given Jenny a glass of water and are taking turns using a stethoscope to listen at Jennifer's belly.

"It's very fast!" one girl says to another while passing over the scope.

"Yeah, but not too fast," one of the boys says. "Infant pulses are normally over a hundred beats a minute."

Ken pushes himself out of the chair. "All of you, out. You can listen from the door."

The group of young teens shuffle out with little complaint. "I wouldn't want to watch that anyway," one boy mutters.

"At least we can listen. There will be more babies. Mary must be ready to have hers soon."

I follow the herd, but Jenny grabs my arm as I pass her. "Stay with me?"

I rub a hand over my own belly. I'm still not showing, but Jenny was there for me a week ago, when I needed her. "Of course." I'm sure watching her is going to freak me out, especially if it takes twenty hours, but I might as well know what I'm in for. I lace my fingers through hers and squeeze gently.

She squeezes my hand back and takes a shaky breath. She's scared, I realize. "You're going to be fine," I remind her. "You and Patience."

"Patience?" she asks. I curse quietly. "That's a nice name."

"I didn't mean to tell you. You should name her whatever you think fits."

"I like Patience." She's looking better again, as is Kenny, who is taking her blood pressure. Then he lays a sheet over her knees and asks her to slide to the end of the bench.

Grimacing a little, Jenny obeys and Ken sticks his head under the sheet. He pops up a moment later.

"You aren't that close, only a couple inches. If you want to walk around, you should."

Jenny nods and gets down from the bench, tying the robe around her. The crowd at the door parts for us as we begin to pace up and down the hall in front of the infirmary.

“Thank you, Cassy.”

“For what?” Staying here? Why wouldn’t I?

“For warning us. For being here for me. So many people didn’t listen to you, and they aren’t here. You saved us.”

I hate hearing this. “No, I failed. I couldn’t stop the virus at the source. I had all this extra knowledge and what did it do for us? Nothing.”

Jenny shakes her head. “You made do with what you had. You are a hero, Cassy.”

“I think you’re the hero,” I tell her. “You’re willing to be a mother to not just one but hundreds of kids. You’ve stepped up to feed us with the scraps we’re able to raid. You’ve got a garden ready for the spring so we can feed ourselves. You are a hero.”

Jenny blushes but doesn’t argue. She takes a compliment better than I do, the way I used to, the first time. It seems so long ago now that I don’t remember the girl I was then.

Jenny stops, clutching my hand more tightly. She breathes slowly and it's hitched. Eventually, it evens out and she eases up on my hand. "They're getting harder," she says, like I couldn't tell.

"Do you want to turn back?" We've just passed the infirmary in our pacing.

She shakes her head. "I'm still good, I think." She only gets another eight strides before she doubles up again, her face pinching with pain. "Owwowowow!" The cry is almost a wail as it oscillates between frequencies. The verbal cue seems to help pass the pain more quickly, and we're on our way again.

When we reach the infirmary on our return trip, I pull Jenny through the door. The contractions are coming quickly now, every third or fourth minute. Kenny is muttering to himself as he touches tools on a tray. I recognize the scalpel, as does Jenny.

"Just to cut the cord," he assures us. "I hope," he adds in a whisper.

I help Jenny onto the bench and she slides down once more, opening her legs for Kenny. She doesn't bother with the blanket this time, a sign of how much pain she must be in.

Her breathing is heavy and quick and I recognize signs of fatigue, the signs that mean I could fall if another attack comes. Squeezing her hand, I try to help her focus on me. "Breathe, Jenny. In fast, out slow." I show her what I mean, the succession of inhales and a heavy blowing exhale. "Make it as long you can." I show her, blowing long and slow. She can't manage that, but her breathing starts to even out. She doesn't look or sound like she's exhausted.

"You're fully dilated. Do you feel the urge to push?"

Her next exhale is a "HA!" and she nods rather than answer. "Pu-shing," she says on the next exhalation. It's followed by gulping gasping breaths leading to another effort that turns her face dark red. I worry a little about her breaking blood vessels, but only wipe away the hair from her face, blowing lightly on her brow to cool it.

She continues to push, and Kenny encourages her, too.

"That's it, Jenny. She's crowning. Just a few more pushes now. There, I have her head."

My eyes widen and I look at Kenny's hands, at the blood covered cone shape between them. He turns it a little and I can make out a nose, but everything else is just blood and wrinkles.

"Push, Jenny, push out the shoulders. Cassy, grab that towel for me?"

I let go of Jenny's hand to get the large towel. Kenny holds the grotesque-looking head in one hand, while cupping the towel under it with the other. He seems to pull, very slightly. Then the baby slides right out and into the towel. Kenny scoops quickly, the baby nearly slipping from his grasp. Without the towel, I'm pretty sure it would have. His hands are as slick as the infant.

"Here, Cassy," he says as he hands me the towel. I freeze, completely unsure how to hold her. She's so small, so fragile and so ugly. I don't remember Patience being this ugly. Kenny uses the scalpel to cut the cord and motions for me to take the baby to Jenny.

Shaking slightly, I turn very slowly. Jenny already has a smile on her face. “She’s beautiful,” she murmurs, reaching for the bundle in my arms.

Beautiful? She looks worse than some of the meat sacks I’ve killed, but I’m not going to say that. As Jenny uses a corner of the towel to wipe away blood, I see the baby hiding underneath. She isn’t ugly after all. I still wouldn’t call her pretty, not yet, but I know from the first time that she’ll be a roly-poly ball of baby fat in just a week or two.

“Congratulations,” I tell Jenny as Kenny busies himself with extracting the afterbirth.

“Patience,” she murmurs, kissing the baby girl on the head. “You’re right, that’s her name.”

I smile a little sheepishly and wonder what she might have named the baby if I hadn’t told her that. I suppose it doesn’t really matter that much in the larger scheme of things.

“Worried about your turn?” Jenny asks.

I freeze in place. I hadn't thought about me and my baby. I'm going to have to do that, all of that.

"Well, I feel ready," Kenny says with a smile of his own. "That wasn't nearly as bad as I imagined."

I can't help but laugh at him while Jenny's jaw drops. "Not that bad?" she asks in disbelief. "That was terrible!"

"Oh, I didn't mean for you. I worried I would screw up."

Jenny's expression softens quickly and I pat Ken's arm. "I'm sure it'll be more exciting for you next time."

CHAPTER ELEVEN

HEPH IS taking his turn at driving while I sleep in the passenger seat. Noonday sun streams through the windshield, doubly blinding for the snow glare, but I'm oblivious. I've learned to sleep when I can, when I feel safe. In a moving vehicle, with Heph at the wheel, is about as safe as I can get outside Freetown.

"Wake up, Cassy," he says, kissing my nose and tickling me with the hair that he needs to cut again.

"Hmm?" I ask, puckering my lips as I stretch. They land on his stubbly chin.

"We're here," he tells me, moving to open the back doors of the van. We'll leave everything open for our return. We never know what might be chasing us or which direction we could come from. Besides, meat sacks have no use for anything inside, except us.

I stretch once more and feel Heph's eyes following me as I do. He's so easy to tease. "We should hurry," I say as I roll out of the seat. "I don't want to be in town when it gets dark." I sling my rifle over my head and slide my pistol back into its holster.

I will be; that's almost guaranteed. Omaha isn't small and the survivors, if there are any, didn't leave any big signs out. Just like when we found Mary and Joshua, we'll have to search to find them. I'll guard Heph while he sleeps at night, but we'll probably do that in town somewhere rather than returning to the van.

Heph takes the lead, hiking at a good speed into town. It isn't long before we're walking in an awkward shuffle, back to back, picking off meat sacks as they close in around us. I break off and run up the steps toward a bank. The door is unlocked and I pull it open, turning my back to it. I prepare to shoot a way clear for Heph and to hide inside.

I fall forward as something punches into me from behind.

"Cassy!" Heph shouts, dropping fire to run to me. I push myself up on to my elbows, but that only allows me to see him ripped apart by the zombies surrounding him. There's something else in the crowd. A strange red shape.

"Those weren't zombies!"

I continue to push back as hands lift me from the ground and carry me into the bank.

"I don't think she's gonna make it," one of the people holding me says.

I look down at the blood spreading down my abdomen from the bullet wound in my belly.

The baby, I think before blackness envelopes me.

CHAPTER TWELVE

I'M BACK on the beach. I clutch at my middle. Am I still pregnant? I don't think I can be. After all, I've gone back to a time before Heph and I had sex. I'm still a virgin, right? But then what happens to that baby? Did it die when I did? Why didn't it come back as well? Or did it?

The surf rolls in around my legs and I decide that it doesn't matter. Baby or no baby, virus or no virus, I'm not caring this time. I'm going to live for me.

"Cassandra? What's wrong, honey?" Mom asks. But it's not really my mom, she's just a meat sack-in-waiting.

"Nothing," I snap back. "Can we go?"

"I don't like your tone," Dad says, light dancing in his blue eyes. "Entirely inappropriate for vacation."

I can't help but laugh at my Dad's pitiful attempt at humor. "Guess I'm just overheated."

"Sadly, we do need to go," Mom says, frowning.

"Yes, long drive home."

"Can I drive?" I ask.

My parents regard one another before Dad passes me the keys. "Why not?"

As I hope, they both drift off before we've gone far. Putting the hammer down, I race toward Gallup. My parents are still asleep as I blow past our home and on toward Manson in Albuquerque. Abandoning all subtlety, I pull the hand brake, giving both parents a rude awakening.

I leave them in the Caravan, dashing into the building and heading straight for the security office. The guard is in it and not looking too sharp. A few rapid hits with the side of my fist and his gun is in my hand, a bullet in his brain.

This time, killing an aware person doesn't affect me, not like it did when I killed Dr. Evans. This guard is just another inevitable meat sack. I can't stop the virus that would have infected him, but I do want my revenge on as many of the people responsible as I can.

My target shifts to the receptionist, a cleaning lady, an intern. Every white coat turns red without hesitation on my part. I take down another guard and slide his gun between my breasts, keeping the first tight in my grip.

My parents are in the lobby when I start to make my way out of the building. As far as I can tell, there is no one left alive inside.

"Cassy! What have you done?"

I level the pistol at my father's chest and fire.

"No!" my mother screams, falling to her knees beside him. "How could y—" She's cut off with my final bullet. I drop the gun beside them and walk out, my vengeance spent.

Sitting in the Caravan, I start to laugh at the inevitability of everything.

Of course, I'm not satisfied with that. I drive the caravan around a corner just as the lights of a cop car flash in my rearview.

Remembering the route from the second time, I park in the Evans' driveway. Everyone is still awake, their son getting one last drink of water.

I kick in the front door and shoot Peter Evans first, then his wife. I point the gun at the boy for a second and his screaming dies to a whimper. "Mommy?" He turns to the corpse bleeding out on the kitchen tile.

I click the safety on the pistol and shove it into the back of my dress.

"Come with me," I say in my best imitation of Jenny's soothing tone. "I'll take you somewhere safe. What's your name?"

"Cory."

"Hi, Cory. I'm Cassy. Your parents were going to be very sick, but now they'll be just fine."

Fine and dead; exactly what I want in the doctor's case. How had I forgotten their kid? It doesn't matter, the couple would have turned on him eventually. Besides, he could be the son I didn't get to have last time, the third time.

"No booster seat?" Cory asks as I open the door to the Caravan.

I briefly consider stealing the Evans' car. No one will have reported my parents' van but they'll be looking for the Evans. Best to stick with what I have. "Nope. You're big though, you'll be okay, right?"

He grins a little at the compliment, puffing his four-year old chest as I fasten the belt over it before climbing in behind the wheel. As I do, I see lights flashing at the end of the crescent.

"Hold on, Cory," I shout before throwing the van into gear and peeling out.

Cory must be a bit delirious with shock because he starts to laugh rather than cry, not perturbed at all. "Faster!" he shouts, flailing his hands in the air.

The traffic light fifty yards away turns yellow and I give him his wish, jamming the accelerator down just before the cars in the other direction advance. They close behind us, blocking the cops.

“How’re you doing?” I ask a few turns later, looking over my shoulder at Cory in the back seat. He’s passed out, his blond hair mashed against the seatbelt. I take a highway exit and choose a direction I’ve never gone, northeast. I can’t outrun the infection, I can’t stop its spread, but I can see and do a few things before I have to hide or fight for my life.

I pull off at an all-night truck stop to gas up and catch some sleep. We just crossed the border into Oklahoma, somewhere I’ve never been. I’m wiped and crash. It seems way too early when Cory is chattering in my ear.

“Where are we? Where are we going? Can I have something to eat? I’m hungry, and thirsty, and I have to—” He cuts off and starts to whimper as the acrid smell of urine reaches my nose.

"Oh, Cory, really? Outside. Just outside the van you can pee." I reach past him to open the door and spin him around. He's already pulled it out and the dribble splashes on the running board rather than the upholstery.

Cory is crying now, red-faced.

"It's okay. Don't cry. You didn't hurt anything."

He doesn't pull his pants up before hugging my legs. I reach for the back waistband of his pajamas and yank them. It's then that I realize neither of us has a change of clothes. My picture is probably flashing in every cop shop in the country, but I have to go shopping.

"Buckle up, Cory. We're going to Wal-Mart."

My mom's purse and credit cards sit under the passenger seat, making my task that much easier. I could have wasted every soon-to-be meat sack in the big box, but that seemed needlessly risky; much better to just breeze through, grab a few changes for each of us, and wait for the apocalypse to make future purchases unnecessary.

“Can I sit there?” Cory asks, pointing at the front of the cart. I could kiss him.

“You got it, kid. Want me to push fast?” I ask with a menacing grin. He does, and I sprint over the open pavement into the barely open store. It’s still early in the morning, so the place is practically empty, making it easy to race through aisles and grab at whim. My size is easy, but what do I get for a four year old? I end up seizing on 6X and figuring we can roll them up if need be. The credit card goes through fine, and we’re back on the road in no time.

“Spider-man! Spider-man!” Cory sings in the back seat, obviously happy with my choices. I can’t help but smile with him. What are we doing? For the first time, my goals aren’t clear. Once the goal was be popular, then stay alive. God, was I really that shallow back then? I can’t deny, based on the friends I kept at the time that I was. I’m not anymore. Death and destruction will do that. I am feeling very frivolous at the moment. I’ve tried saving the world twice now, and it seems obvious I’m not going to succeed, so

I'm going to live. I'm going to enjoy this time for as long as I can.

"Ever seen the Statue of Liberty, Cory?" I ask. I haven't and it's about time I did, isn't it? "We can see the UN and maybe the Empire State Building."

"King Kong!" he shouts in excitement.

I turn and look over my shoulder. "You watched King Kong?" Who would let a kid watch that?

He claps his hands and starts making plane propeller noises. I can't help but grin.

"That's right. We'll stay on the inside, okay?" I tell him, selecting the exit to take us there.

Just after one of our many pit-stops—did I pee this much when I was a kid?—I spy cop lights behind me. Changing exits, I lose them in a little town I've never heard of before. However, I take advantage of the opportunity to pull over and give Cory some out-of-car time at a park. Playing with the other kids, there's nothing to suggest that we're anything other than siblings or cousins enjoying the summer day. Pulling my shades over my eyes, I lounge on one of the benches and nod off.

I'm woken by a screeching. "Ow! Oweee! Ow!!" I straighten quickly and jostle the mother next to me holding an infant.

"He just skinned his knee," she assures me, smiling.

"Okay, Cory, let me see. It's not even bleeding," I tell him.

"Band-Aid?" he asks.

"If I get you a band-aid, we have to get back in the car."

He holds his cries for a moment, obviously considering. "Yes, band-aid."

I ruffle his hair. "Okay then. There's a first aid kit in the van. Thanks for letting me snooze," I tell the woman next to me.

"No problem. They were all having fun." Taking Cory's tiny hand in mine we walk back to the van. An idea strikes me before I leave. Pulling up behind another grey caravan, one that looks almost identical to mine, I swap license plates. Well, I don't swap so much as take theirs and leave mine in the trash. The cops will have the new one quick enough, but then it has to go through all the channels again. I won't have to hide long. The infection will already be spreading.

We spend our nights at truck stops, sleeping in the van. I always park with our rear against another truck or car, hiding the plate. A caravan at a truck stop isn't unusual or remarkable and no one should find us. Cory is asleep by the time I park and close my eyes, and in the morning he wakes me up. My only companion on this mad journey that helps no one but myself. Not even him.

We've pulled off in three other towns, I've stolen three more plates, and Cory has made a lot of friends he'll never see again. It's only when I see one kid watching a show in the back of his van that I remember ours has a DVD in the back. Grinning, I stop at another Wal-Mart and stock up on movies for the boy. The supply lets me stop once at a park each day instead of twice.

More days pass and Cory starts to whine about his parents and going home. The farther we go, the more I wonder why I did what I did. I haven't warned anyone. I killed a lot of people. And for what? A joy-ride with a four-year-old?

That's exactly it. I've given up and I'm enjoying my last days before the apocalypse, except I'm not enjoying them. For the first time, I'm lonely. I've killed my parents and run away from Heph and Jenny and the future that held them. Instead, I'm spending my last days with a boy who can't hold his pee for more than a minute.

Speaking of him, I glance in rearview where Cory, full on his happy meal, is passed out. I kick up the speed again. Fighting desperate thoughts, futile tears, I decide I will be happy. I am going to see things I've never seen before, and when the time comes, I will hide and fight and try to survive just as I have every time before. I decide I'm not going to care about anyone else.

But I do care. I care that Heph will have to kill his parents to escape again. I care that Jenny survives and has Patience. I do care that I killed my parents. I shot them.

I pull over, swerving, as tears flood my vision. I see my parents clearly, for the first time since I began this mad journey, bleeding on the floor. I remember all the other people, the Manson staff, the Evans. Fighting the tears back, I pull onto the highway again, planning to stop at the next truck stop for a good cry. I might even try to smuggle out something to drink to ease my guilt.

***

New York is a lot bigger than I expect. One more potty break gives me a chance to pick up a map while Cory chows down on an order of fries.

“Cassy?”

“Yeah, Cory?”

“When are we going home?”

I look up from my map to see him looking at me expectantly. This isn’t the first time he’s asked. It’s not even the first time he’s asked today. His mouth and cheeks are shining with grease from the fries.

"Mom and Dad are okay now, right?" he asks.

I did tell him that.

"Yeah, but we can't go home yet. We haven't gotten to see the Empire State Building. I'm figuring out how to get there, see?" I hold up the map.

"Oh, and then we'll go home?"

"Sure, kid," I say noncommittally, studying the map again. By the time we're done sight-seeing, it should be obvious, even to a four-year-old, that there is no home anymore.

The monuments are less than I expect, less than I'm hoping for; a disappointment. I killed people and ran away for this? They're big, and beautiful, and old, but the people they're meant to commemorate, or honor, or inspire are all going to be mindless monsters in a few hours. Even the people visiting, coming and going, are all meat-sacks-in-waiting.

We're in the elevator on our way down from the top of the Empire State Building when I run a suggestion past Cory.

"Hey, kid, how would like to see where the President lives?"

"Yeah!" he says excitedly.

There's no way I'm getting into the White House, but we can at least visit. Maybe I can watch the great Capitol fall apart as the virus takes all of them.

"Cassy? I'm hungry."

"Again?" I ask. This kid is a bottomless pit.

"Yeah, but can I have something good this time? Like pah-sketti?"

I laugh. "You're actually tired of eating McDonald's? I didn't think any kid got tired of that."

He makes a face. "No more."

I laugh harder. "Sure, kid. Let's get something really good." Instead of loading back in the van, I walk hand-in-hand with Cory down Fifth Avenue. Empire Pizza seems a likely place for spaghetti and Cory gets a big plate to himself while I take a slice, expecting to eat left overs.

He surprises me, packing away all the pasta and making me buy a second slice. However, instead of happy and full, he whines as soon as we load back into the van.

"Do I have to sleep in here again? Can't we go home?"

"Nope, we're going to see the President," I remind him, "but we can sleep outside." I'm pretty sure it isn't going to rain tonight. I remember a map full of suns from my repeated loops.

"Yay! Camping!" He buckles up with a smile now. Once more he's asleep before we've gone far. This kid loves sleeping on the road. He wakes when I pull off the highway. He's all keen to lie back and count stars. I try to count with him, but my usual nocturnal nature isn't part of this body's rhythm yet, and I fall asleep listening to his little voice, "fo-teen, fifteen, sis-teen, seventeen......"

A loud honking from another vehicle wakes me and I find a man in uniform standing over me.

"Shit."

"Bad word!" Cory says. I look around for him and see he's holding the hand of another officer. He has strands of grass in his hair.

"Cassandra Jacobs?"

"Yeah, that's me." I climb to my feet and rake my fingers through my hair, getting caught on the long locks. Damn, didn't I cut that this time?

The officer turns me, not gently, and cuffs my hands behind my back.

"They're going to take us home, Cassy." Cory is still excited and smiling.

"Yeah, sure they are, Cory," I mutter. The officer's hands are very warm, clammy. I look over my shoulder, sure of what I'll find. His eyes are starting to glaze. He's already a goner. I look to his partner holding Cory. He's a little better off. He's flushed, but his eyes are still clear. "You guys don't look so good," I say. "You coming down with something?"

"Just keep quiet," the one holding me says, pushing me into the backseat with Cory.

"Sure, just make sure you stop when he says. He doesn't kid around about needing to pee."

The more lucid of the pair chuckles at that. "No kid does. Y' know, she's right, Mark, you don't look good. Want me to drop you off?"

“I’m fine,” Mark says gruffly. “Let’s take them in.”

“We’re taking them back to Albuquerque, remember?” Mark’s partner asks. “I am dropping you off.”

“No, you are not! They aren’t taking me alive!” He unsnaps the latch on his pistol holster.

His mind is gone, making him spew gibberish. I’ve already pulled my knees to my chest, so I’m just sliding my hands front when Mark shoots his partner. Then he collapses atop him, mouth wide open as the injured man continues to fight and flail. Cory’s lip trembles at the bang, but he’s too low on the seat to see what happened just outside my window. Luckily, Mark’s partner hadn’t closed the door on Cory’s side so I jump out, slam the door behind me and hop in the front.

“Ever ride in a cop car, Cory?”

His lip stops trembling at my grin. He couldn’t see anything and takes assurance from my expression. He smiles back, probably thinking the bang was thunder or something. “No! Yay!” He’s so easy to please. I lock the door just as Mark is trying to puzzle out how to get the meat out of the can—the meat being us and the car the can. Fumbling with the key ring in the ignition, I manage to open my cuffs. Reversing, I nearly take Mark's arm off, but we're long gone before he can find his feet and chase after us. In the rear view, I see him pull a trucker from the same pullout through the window of his cab. The driver was probably infected too.

I do head for Washington, hoping to find some cache of survivors locking themselves away.

"Cassy, where is Mom?"

I grind my teeth. "Want me to turn on the siren again?" I ask Cory.

"No, I want Mom."

"Cory, we can't go home. There isn't a home to go to anymore."

"Yes, there is! It's where I live with Mom and Dad."

"You don't have a mom or dad anymore, Cory."

"Yes, I do!" he argues emphatically. "I want to go home!"

I try being reasonable. "Look, your mom and dad got sick just like that policeman. You remember what happened to him?"

"No."

I close my eyes and count to ten. Surprisingly, it works. It never used to work. "He ate the other policeman. Your parents would have eaten you."

"No." I look at him briefly and he's pouting.

"We're going to Washington, Cory. I'm going to try and find somewhere safe for us to stay, okay?"

"Good. I don't want to drive anymore."

I can't blame him there. I'm going nuts while my bum is slowly falling asleep. The roads are quiet, another sign that the infection is affecting more and more people. In Washington, I head toward the White House only because I don't know where to go. How do I find a cell when they are probably just gathering? Also, they'll want to be well hidden as more and more adults start losing their minds.

I'm in luck. I spot a boy with a rifle on his back. He's dressed normally otherwise, just has a rifle over his shoulder. He's one of the only people on the street.

"Where are you going?" I ask.

He narrows his eyes at me, uncertain he should answer.

"I'm looking for somewhere to hole up," I explain. "I've got a kid with me. He needs somewhere safe. Neither of us are infected." That's actually a lie; we're all infected, just immune. It's what the kid needs to hear.

"We're next door to the Library of Congress." He walks to the passenger door and gets in beside me. "How'd you snag a cop car?"

"What are you doing walking down the street?"

"Raiding supplies. There are still enough lucid adults that we have to be careful not to steal from the same place twice."

I nod in understanding. It's the reason I only bought what we needed at Wal-Mart. The end will come soon enough. He points and I turn down a different road.

"How many are you?" I ask.

"There are forty of us so far, but we expect more as more parents go nuts."

He's right. "And you're set up to stay in this building? You've removed all the adults, of course."

"Of course. Who are you anyway?"

I take a deep breath before answering. "I'm from Albuquerque, ground zero. I was in the Manson building the day of the outbreak."

"You're Cassandra Jacobs!" he says in sudden realization. "Everyone is looking for you. You killed twenty people that day. Including your parents!" He's shouting at me now and I resist the urge to punch him to settle him down.

"Pleasure. And you are?"

"Oh, yeah, I'm Danny. You really opened fire on an entire building?"

"A building of soon-to-be meat sacks," I mutter.

"What's he talking about, Cassy?" Cory asks from behind us.

"Nothing important, kid. We'll be there soon. Right?" I ask Danny.

"Huh? Oh, yeah, just a few more blocks. You are wanted, how are you in a cop car?"

"The officers turned on each other."

"Oh," Danny mutters in quiet understanding. "At least you got away."

I nod my agreement. "This is Cory, by the way. He's a good kid."

"Hi, Cory, I'm Danny."

"I want to go home," Cory announces again, returning to his pout.

"We are going home," I try to explain again. "Your home isn't there anymore. Your mom and dad aren't waiting for you."

"He's not...Cory Evans?"

I glance out of the corner of my eye at Danny who is still dumbstruck.

"You kidnapped the doctor's kid?"

"I didn't kidnap him. I orphaned him. Seems only right that I make sure he's okay, doesn't it?"

"Seems a little nuts to me. Why would you want to be weighed down with kid while you're on the run?"

"I don't want that, but we are going to need kids in the long run, and Cory didn't do anything to deserve what would have happened if I'd left him behind. So, we're going sight-seeing together, right Cory?"

"We went to the Empire State Building!" He claps his hands in delight.

"That's right. Where else did we go?"

"The Statue of Liberty."

"Let me get this straight," Danny begins, "you've been out sight-seeing while the infection is spreading."

"That's right," I snap back. "You have a problem with that? What would you have me do? Shoot more people?"

"Maybe..." He doesn't sound certain at all. "Why Manson? How did you know?"

"I just did, okay? How much further?"

"Oh, it's right here," he says pointing at a cement structure with tall thin windows on each side. I have to smile at the sight of it. No meat sack is getting in there easily.

"Great spot," I murmur.

"Thanks. Getting the representatives out was a bit of a problem, but most of them headed to their home districts as soon as word of the infection got out."

I'm not really listening as I pull up to a gate. A girl with a rifle stands there and Danny sticks his head out to shout at her.

"Hey! It's me. Let us in."

There's a little more back and forth before she pushes a button and retracts the gate.

"So, why D.C.?" Danny asks as I find a place to park the car. I leave the keys on the dash.

I shrug. "Seemed a likely place for a few military minded kids to set up." I open the back door for Cory.

"Pee?" he asks, holding himself.

"Just go behind the door," I mutter, shaking my head. He hides a little behind the open door of the car.

"How did you know?" Danny asks again. "The news was full of you for days, until the infection spread. Then it was all about Manson and Peter Evans' experiment gone wrong. They figure you bought everyone a couple of days by taking out so many of the infected. Did you know that?"

I shake my head. "Nope, don't care either."

"But you had to have known. Why else would you go on a bender there, and then go to Evans' home and kill him? What do you know?"

I lose it. "Yes, I saw it all coming and just couldn't take it, okay? They'd all turned so many times that I just wanted to get some of them before they were a problem. I wanted to feel less defeated."

"You saw it?" Danny asks hesitantly.

"Forget it, okay? I had a weird sixth sense and took care of it. It's done now." He wasn't buying it, and Cory had finished his tinkle. "Come on, kid, I'm not sure we want to stay here." I start pushing him back into the car.

"No, wait, Cassy," Danny says. "You are welcome here. Have you seen anything else? Anything that can help us?"

I sigh heavily. "A group of cadets is going to take Fort Carson and set up a zombie-free zone.

The immune from across the country are going to gather there."

"Sweet!" Danny says with a fist pump. "You need to tell the others that. We'll be on our way there in no time!"

I cock an eyebrow. Does he really think they'll just believe me? Every time I've gone through this someone doubts, someone can't accept that I have the knowledge I have, someone holds the rest back.

"We'll see," I say. "You ready to go meet a new family, Cory?"

"I want my family!"

"That's what this is." I kneel in front of him, trying to engage him. I've seen Jenny do this sometimes. "All the adults are sick, Cory. None of them can be in our family anymore. I don't have a mom or dad anymore either. They're with your mom and dad now, where we can't get them back. But there is a new family here for us, a family of other kids. We're going to be okay if we stick together. Can you do that? Can you stick with us?"

He sways on the spot for a moment, not wanting to answer. Finally, he lets out a heavy breath. “Okay, Cassy.”

Smiling, I give him a hug and then take his hand as we follow Danny out of the underground parking. Looking around, I see more than enough vehicles to get all of us to Fort Carson. I know people came from DC the second time, when Heph and I got the word out, but I can’t remember if anyone did the first time. In any case, forty or even a hundred kids shouldn’t strain Freetown like the second time.

“Tell me why you were walking again?” Surely, he could have taken one of these cars.

“Would you believe none of us knows how to hot wire a car? That’s the problem with being the kids of a bunch of politicians and diplomats.”

I can’t help but laugh. “No, it makes sense. I didn’t know how either. I do now. No more risking ourselves by walking around.”

Danny’s grin widens, his teeth bright against his darker skin. “Perfect. I’m so glad you came, Cassy.”

I'm not, but I don't know how to explain that. I gave up this time. I didn't even try to help anyone besides myself. I could have been trying to figure out what set off the virus. I could have tried to warn people again, without naming Freetown. Maybe I could have set up some sort of bunker for uninfected adults where we left food for them in an airlock, just like Kenny's mice. Instead, I shot up a bunch of people and went sight-seeing. I haven't grown up at all, have I?

"Something wrong?" Danny asks from the stair above me. The elevators have already jammed.

"No. I'm good."

"I'm ti-ired." Cory complains around a yawn.

"Hop on," I say, turning to face down the stairwell so he can hop onto my back.

"Yay! Piggy back." Were the kids in Freetown this easy to make happy? Or is Cory just a naturally happy kid? I can't really fault him wanting to go home, I want to go home too. Every little distraction I try to use to make it easier for him, he laps up and makes seem that much bigger and better than I intend. He really is a good kid.

"We're going to stick together, right Cory? You and me."

"Yep. Love you, Cassy." He hugs tight around my neck and I feel almost as sure of myself as I do when Heph hugs me or slaps my shoulder in appreciation.

Stupid contacts are making my eyes bleary. I didn't stop at home for my glasses this time. I wipe at them with my fingers and pull them out. I don't need them except to drive anyway. That and shoot long, but I'll find glasses.

Danny leads us to a large room with a gigantic table in the middle. It's actually several tables slid together, I see as I get closer. There are chairs all around it, easily fifty or sixty.

"Danny, what do you have for us?" one of the girls asks, looking at Cory and me.

"This is Cassandra Jacobs and Cory Evans."

"Bullshit," one of the boys cusses. Then he squints at me. "Holy crap, it is her!"

“Bad words!” Cory shouts, his mouth going into an O.

“Do you have any scissors?” I ask, keeping my voice as neutral as possible, hoping Cory won’t go too crazy about the bad words. “I’d really like to cut my hair.”

“I can do it for you,” the girl who spoke first offers. “I’m Melissa. Have a seat.” She motions to the many chairs.

“No food?” the skeptical boy asks. Remembering that most of the kids here are probably children of diplomats, he might actually be from India, or Iran, or something. He has black hair and brown skin.

Danny frowns. “No, I brought her back instead. Oh, but get this, she had a cop car. So, I’ll take that out. Maybe go as far as Arlington.”

“She brought a cop car?” he asks, still skeptical. “You are one badass,” he says to me. I’m holding my head steady while Melissa cuts off my locks. She clicks her tongue as she does, probably envious of my hair and thinking I’m nuts to cut it.

"Whatever," I answer. "I'm just informed."

"Yeah, about that, how did you know?"

"And you are?" I ask, not wanting to start spouting to just anyone.

"In charge. Start talking, sister."

I let half a minute go by, just to make it clear that I don't buy his assumed authority. I've been wary of older kids since the second time when those in their twenties started sending the rest of us into more and more dangerous situations.

"I know because I've done this before, several times. I keep getting sent back to do it again. So I know that every person over the age of twenty-five is going to lose their mind and turn cannibal. Most people under twenty-five, but not all, will be immune, and we will have to band together if we want any hope of preserving humanity as we knew it."

That's a rather large pill for anyone to swallow and the skeptic isn't even trying.

"Yeah, sure. I think you just had a bad side effect and decided to take it out on Manson."

I shrug. He can believe whatever he likes.

“She said there’s going to be a gathering in Fort Carson, a whole town where kids will gather,” Danny explains.

“She said. I don’t much care about what she said.”

“Check online. Go Army. They’ve probably got the message up already. It won’t be there long. Power will start failing in a few days.” I pause, thinking. “I don’t remember when it goes out here. Twenty-eighth? Twenty-ninth? Somewhere in there.”

The boy pulls out his phone and starts punching information into it.

He huffs. “She’s right. It’s right here. Be Free in Fort Carson. Okay, Cassandra, let’s go.”

“Not yet,” I tell him. “More people will come out and we want to take all of them with us.”

“How are we going to move more people?” Melissa asks. “We don’t have vehicles for the ones we have.”

“I can hotwire the rest,” I tell them. “I won’t promise they’ll work for more than a couple of wirings. It really fries the on-board computers.

It's best for old cars, but I can start anything once."

"How long do you expect us to stay?" the skeptic asks.

"You really won't tell me your name?" I ask.

After a few moments Melissa sighs, "He's Ahmed, and he's a pain in the ass."

"I can tell."

"How long?" he asks through clenched teeth.

"Three days. That will be enough time so that anyone who is going to escape will and anyone who can't will have fallen. I don't know if you've noticed, but they prefer uninfected meat."

Everyone nods around the table at that. "Well, you might as well meet some of the others," Melissa suggests with a smile.

"Here, take Cory. I'm going to head out again with Danny. Got a gun I can take with me?"

Melissa and Ahmed look at each other. "No," she says finally. "All of the ones we have are already assigned."

I nod. "No big. Where's the biggest knife in the place? I'll make do until I can find something better."

Eyes go wide. "You fight with a knife?" Ahmed says slowly, even more incredulous than before.

"Obviously, I would prefer not to let them get that close, but yes. I can drop one to the ground with bare hands if I have to. You should learn how."

"I'll get you a knife," Melissa murmurs, leaving the meeting room.

"I don't know who you are, Cassy, but I'm starting to think I'm glad you came here, too." Ahmed admits reluctantly. He reminds me of Joshua and a hundred others that didn't believe me, but couldn't deny in the face of all the evidence. If he saw me fight a meat sack with a knife, the way Joshua did, he'd be even less reluctant than he is now.

"I'm hungry," Cory says, breaking the silence that has hung since Melissa left.

I look at Ahmed.

"Yeah, come with me." He leads the way from the board room. I don't move to follow and Danny stops to look at me.

"We should wait here for Melissa," I tell him. "Then we can get more food."

"Right."

"No! Cassy, don't go!" Cory runs from Ahmed to cling to my legs. "I want to go with you."

I rub the boy's back. "You'll be fine here Cory. Ahmed will get you something to eat and introduce you to some people you can play with."

"I don't want to play with them," he says sullenly. "I want to play with you."

"I can't play right now, Cory. I need to go get more food so you have something to eat. You're hungry, right?"

"Yeah," he whines, still pouting. "But I don't want you to go."

"I'll be back," I promise, kissing the top of his head.

"Okay." He reluctantly releases me and follows Ahmed. So slowly in fact, that Melissa returns within moments of them leaving. Danny's barely gotten his fanboy on again, but I can see it in his brown eyes. They dance when they look at me, like I'm some sort of heroine from a story. I wish.

"Thanks, Melissa," I say, taking the heavy hunting knife from her. "Nice," I murmur as I flip it a few times. It's weighted properly for throwing, not that I'd be stupid enough to throw my only blade. "Ready, Danny?"

"Yep!" He jumps to follow me.

"Good, 'cause I'm taking your rifle and you're driving." I pull the strap from his shoulder.

"What?"

"I don't know my way around here. You do. Let's see how much we can fit in that car trunk and backseat." I grin, thinking ahead to the raid. Looting is not stealing. Stealing implies someone else owned or in another way claimed the goods. Anyone who could have been said to own the stock in the store isn't aware enough to know we're taking it.

Danny parks in front of a Safeway and I lean out of the car door, aiming and firing his rifle as quickly as I can. A whole gang of meat sacks have noticed our entrance and believe us fair game. A bullet to the brain does wonders for changing that perception.

He's still sitting beside me for some reason. "Go!" I shout, shoving him into motion. "I'll hold them off as long as I can."

He jumps up and runs into the store through the automatic doors. They're probably unlocked from last night.

I try to pick my targets more carefully, knowing I don't have a ton of ammo. "Hurry!" I shout, hoping Danny can hear me inside. If he doesn't load the car soon, there won't be any cover fire when he does try.

A rattle behind me of shopping carts makes me turn. There is another boy in a Safeway apron pushing a second cart. I fire my last bullets as they open the trunk.

"Arrr!" I growl running into the pack with my knife. Hooking the arm of one monster, his head hanging limply down his back, I attempt to wear him like a shield. I have to protect my back somehow, but his weight throws me off balance, and trying to keep him there restricts my ability to strike out with my knife.

I have dozens of bites on my arms and legs when I hear the car engine. Chucking the body off me, I fight my way out of the crush, gaining more bites and losing more blood. Throwing myself through the back door that Danny has left open for me, I pull it shut and he peels away, running over a female as he does.

"Holy crap. Did we really make it out of there? I thought we were all dead." The Safeway employee is looking over his seat. "Um, Dan, I don't think she's gonna make it." Everything is already going dark as more and more blood pours out of me onto the seat. I can still hear them, but they are faint. There's something red over my eyes.

"Tell Cory, he's a good kid."

I slip out of consciousness and then out of life.

Chapter Thirteen

SITTING ON the beach again, I can't help but feel guilty for wasting the last time, the fourth time. I look up from the sea foam, intent on restricting the spread of the virus as much as I can, buying as many days for as many Freetowns as possible. That means being subtle. No shooting sprees, instead I'll aim for silent stabbings in alleys. It also means getting word out, specific words, and plans. That means I'm going to need Heph.

Did I really go through the entire fourth time without talking to him, seeing him? I feel that keenly now, desperate for his voice, his face. I won't see him soon, not physically, and it will be a week before I can call him on his phone, but I will find him and others online.

I have an idea now who will listen and who will scoff. My reach will be more precise. I will buy us all the time we need.

"You going to sit there all day?" Dad asks. Dad, not a meat sack. I'm going to buy them time too. Try to get them the first adult enclosure. But where? Inside Carson? A bomb shelter? Are there any of those still around? There must be. They'll have to find them, shut themselves in. Will they believe me?

"Cassy? Are you okay?" Mom asks as several more minutes pass without me moving or answering. I'm making and changing plans, intent on making this the time I save the most people, the time I don't die trying. Set cells in power plants, keep things running. If a boiler room can be a defended stronghold, a power plant can. More people, the right people.

"Sorry, Mom, distracted. Is it time to go already?" I ask wistfully, knowing it is, knowing what I have to do tonight and tomorrow. I need to let my parents know where I'm going and why. What they can and should do to save themselves. Maybe they won't believe me and assume I ran away, but they need to know.

I start writing in my Day-Timer in the back of the Caravan. It's from school and yet still empty. I never used it. I start with my plans, fleshing them out. Then I write the letter:

Mom and Dad,

I'm leaving for Albuquerque in the morning to take a job on the cleaning staff at Manson. A doctor there has created a super virus that is going to infect everyone over twenty-five and turn them into monsters. I know this because I've seen it happen four times. Every time you attack me and my friends at my birthday party, unless I kill you first. That isn't going to happen this time. I'm going to kill all of the members of Dr. Evans's team to slow the spread. You will have time to lock yourselves away somewhere. The virus is airborne but can't live without a host. If you hear three knocks on your door, wait twenty-four hours and then open it. Someone is bringing you supplies.

Stay safe. I love you.

Cassy

I spend the entire night on my computer, logging into every multiplayer shooter game I can find, showing my skills and sending people to my new blog. So far, it's just me gloating and egging guys to take me on. When the infection hits the news, I will post directions, instructions. Several still won't believe, but some will.

In the early morning, a few hours before dawn, I sleep, setting my alarm for six so I can leave before Mom or Dad get up. That will leave me plenty of time to drive to Manson and land my cleaning job. Tonight, I will kill Peter Evans on his way home, then one of his lab assistants each day after, and two staff members a day after that. The death tally rolls in my head but is still nothing compared to my cumulative meat sack count. I do not include my shooting spree the last time, the fourth time. I will not include the Manson employees. They are all people, for now.

The plan is daunting and my sleep is fraught, but I jump at my alarm. I stop to get my hair cut before my interview, which is a breeze again. I pick up a hunting knife from a camping outfitters before my shift, and slip it into my pocket.

As I'm moving through the floors, I notice Evans slip into a bathroom and park my cart in front while dodging in after him.

"Oh!" the doctor says. "I'll just be a moment, then I'll get out of your way."

"Thank you, sir," I answer automatically. Then I lift my head, looking straight into his green eyes. This is probably the only chance I'll ever have to speak to the architect of our destruction, the only chance to tell him what he has done.

"Actually, doctor, you aren't going anywhere. You made a terrible mistake and right now you are carrying it in your blood, spreading it. I can't let you do that."

Lashing out as Heph taught me, I toss the taller, heavier man over my hip and to the floor. His eyes are wide in surprise as I kick him in the side of the head. They close immediately. Holding his head over the toilet, I slit his throat, all the blood flushing away. I then clean the stall and the one adjacent before wedging Evans's body into the bowl, leaving him to be found in the morning. I push my cart down the hall, finishing my hours so I can find a cafe with a computer to rent and log on again.

I shoot up a bunch of cocky boys; boys who have never held a gun, never shot a person. But they will, if they believe me and save themselves. When I can't keep my eyes open any longer, I lock myself in the Taurus and sleep, sure that no meat sacks are coming for me tonight.

I'm not there when they discover Dr. Evans in the morning, but I do hear all about it from my fellow janitorial staff that night. I get to know more of them, holding the job longer. Jane, a girl only a little older than me, thinks one of his assistants did it.

"They're trying to take credit for his work if you ask me. He's working on a cure for cancer. They say it eats the cancer cells without touching any of the healthy ones."

I just smile and nod, knowing it doesn't do anything of the sort. I also follow one of the assistants out of the building toward his car. I don't give him any final words of wisdom to let him know what he has wrought. I just leave him in his car. Cleaning the lab, I find the rabbits and rats. They've started feeding on each other and I can't bear to watch. Using my knife, I kill those and dispose of the bodies as well. If they're changing, the first meat sacks can show up any day now. I skip the taunting game portion of the night and try to sleep for the last night I expect I'll be able.

Evans had four assistants, so when I dispatch the last, I give Heph a call. I try not to be as cagey as the second time; after all, he has met me online.

"Hello?"

"Is this Heph?"

"Yeah, who's this?"

"Seeress."

"No way! How'd you get my number?"

"You gave it to me. A long time ago. Listen, I need some help online. I need someone who knows a lot of people and can spread word fast."

"You're not far off yourself, you know that? Where did you learn to play like that?"

"You don't want to know."

"The hell I don't. Tell me."

"You taught me."

"Bullshit."

"Yeah, it's bullshit. Listen, want to hear something even crazier? Manson Pharmaceuticals has bred a virus that is going to melt the brain of every adult on the planet. Think you can help me convince all the kids to hole up in the power plants with guns?"

"You're kidding, right?"

"I wish. I just killed and then autoclaved a dozen rabbits that were eating each other. It's going to start happening to people soon. I got the first of the infected, but Manson staff are going to go next. Anyone over twenty-five is at risk. Some people under that will go, but not many. We can save all the kids."

"You're full of crap, Seeress."

"Why do you think I picked that handle, KnightRider? Because I've seen it. It's happened before and it's going to happen again. I'm going to post instructions on my blog. Just point people there, okay?"

"Well, I can do that. I have been already. I can't believe no one's been able to take you down."

"They have, Heph, four times already. I'd rather not make it five."

"What do you mean?"

"Nothing, just do this for me? Please?"

"Sure. I can do that. So, you really are a girl. That's not just a handle."

I can't help but laugh. "You're wondering what I look like, aren't you?"

"Well, yeah!"

"I'm cuter than you think."

I hang up on that thought. It'll keep him interested. I can't do more until he's no longer grounded, or he kills his parents. Hopefully, this time, it'll be the former. I hate thinking about Heph locked in his house while his parents lose their minds. The infection is restricted this time, that won't happen before the end of his sentence.

Not for the first time I wonder what he did to get his phone taken away for a week and a further two weeks restricted to the house or outings with family. His step-mom knows how to hit where it hurts, but I've also been told she's fair. He had to have done something really awful for such a huge punishment, but he has never given me the slightest indication what it was.

It can't possibly be as bad as serial killing. I make a stop on my way home at the Evans' house. I imagine Mrs. Evans is having trouble managing without her husband, grieving. Cory seems pretty normal. His father's death probably doesn't seem real to him, thinking he just went on a trip or something. Kids do that, I know. I've listened to Jenny try to explain time and again that their parents aren't coming for them at the end of the day. That they aren't in day care, they're orphans. Cory isn't an orphan, yet. On the other hand, I know Mrs. Evans is infected. As soon as she falls sick, I'm snatching that boy again. He's a good kid and doesn't deserve to be eaten by his mother.

Locking my doors, I curl up, half-alert for banging on the door. I'm not disturbed and rise a little after the sun even though my shift isn't until much later. The news on the radio is the disappearances of Manson staff, the complete loss of one lab.

"Disappearances." I must be doing well in spreading the carnage and bodies if they aren't being billed as murders. That, or Albuquerque doesn't want its citizens thinking it's the sort of place with a murder rate. I must have doubled or tripled it in this week alone. It's going to get worse. Now that the lab is taken care of, I can't discriminate. I have to watch for every bleary eye, every sweaty brow. The first sign of infection and I have to remove them. Arriving early, I see three in the lobby alone. I follow them out into the parking lot and kill one in her car. I cut the brake line of another while he's swooning behind the wheel. He won't make it home. The last I lure into my car and dump the body in a park; anything to mask the trails and make it a little harder to link the deaths. The only commonality should be Manson. I've killed them in different ways, left them in different places. Some probably haven't been found.

I'm beat when I grab my cart and move toward the elevator. Jane joins me.

"You look trashed. What were you doing last night?"

I snort, she probably won't believe me. "Computer games."

"Oh yeah? I'm addicted to a couple of those. Which ones do you play?"

We swap some names and discover that we've run into each other online, hardly surprising the way I've been spreading myself around. I make plans to run into her online again tonight. She mentions that she's been checking out my blog and hopes to find more strategy and less boasting.

I chuckle. "Yeah, there'll be some good tips and tricks there soon, promise."

"Don't you think it's weird how empty the building is? I mean, I know it's night and supposed to be empty, but these eggheads work at all hours, obsessed. Where are they?"

I just shrug and head in another direction. I don't want to talk to her anymore. I don't want to think about where they are, why they aren't here. It has to be done. I can't stop now, even when every murder feels like a layer of grime I can't scrub off my skin.

I need a shower. I make plans to stop at the pool tomorrow. Until then, I'll just feel disgusting. The pool won't actually help with that, just make me physically clean.

***

"Hello?"

"Heph?"

"Seeress."

I chuckle. "Yeah. What are you doing tonight?"

"Nothing. What are you doing?"

"Leveling up."

"Right, I should have known. So, what do you want? The hit count on your blog not high enough?"

I smile. "No, that's doing great. Thanks for your help."

"Then what?"

I actually shrug. "I just wanted to hear your voice. When are you liberated?"

"Why? You want to meet in real life?"

"Yes, I'd like that. You seem like a jerk and I'd like to find out for sure."

"Hey!"

I laugh. "I'm kidding. I want to see if you're as cute as your avatar."

He scoffs. "I'm not. I can tell you that right now."

"Well, you still want to meet me."

"Why?"

"Because I'm even hotter than mine."

"You're killing me, you know that?"

"Yep. So when? Can we make a date?" I suffuse the word with scorn.

"Um, sure, why not. I'm free on the twenty-seventh. Meet for coffee?"

I swallow, my birthday. His parents changed the same day as mine, or earlier. They shouldn't this time, but I have to check.

"How's your family doing? I've heard there's a nasty flu going around. My folks have it."

"There is? I guess a couple people are sick. No, my house is fine."

I sigh with relief. "I'm glad. Sure, I can meet you on the twenty-seventh. How about at the Grinder?" It's a coffee shop in downtown Gallup, just a few blocks from Mr. Brown's ice cream shop.

"You live in Gallup?" he asks, incredulous.

"Actually, yes. Well, I used to. I'm working in Albuquerque this summer, but I can pop in on a weekend." I'd be giving up the job soon, there isn't much more I can do to stem the spread. "I'll see you online."

"You will. I'm taking you down tonight."

"Sure, sure." I hang up, smiling.

Something is bothering me. Something Kenny told me way back, the first time. "There had to be a first specimen infected." He's right, and it is probably the rabbits. Evans didn't inject himself, he breathed in the virus from his animals. Maybe it's both. If there is a next time, and I'm pretty sure there won't be, I will take out the animals as soon as I can.

I can't believe I'm nervous about meeting Heph. He's supposed to meet me at the Grinder at seven. It's six-thirty and I'm parked outside my house, wishing I could go in. I'm infected; that's given. If my parents are still home, they might be as well. I won't be the one that infects them, so I sit outside and hope to see curtains move or lights come on. Nothing, and no Caravan either. Maybe they took my advice. I can hope.

Leaving my car in the driveway, I hit the streets downtown, needing the time to think. I'm a walking incubator for the virus, but enough people here go to Albuquerque on a regular basis that I can't be the only one. How many people are already infected? How many will be infected today? Tomorrow? I imagine a handful of sand running through my fingers into a pile. Everything is the same. I delayed the infection, but it will be just as exponential when it takes hold. Will people believe me if I warn them now? Can I afford to wait?

A car honks and I realize just how dazed I've become. I nearly walked past the Grinder.

"Cassy? Is that Cassy?"

I recognize Julie's voice and duck into a shop, any shop. It's a book store and I feel instantly safe. Julie will never come in here and she will assume anyone who did isn't me. The first time, that would have been true. I'm still not much of a reader, but I don't turn my nose up at it the way I did.

After browsing a shelf, I make my way back out again. I still have a few minutes to get to the Grinder.

Looking through the window, I see Heph sitting at one of the tables looking terribly uncomfortable. His hair is obviously fighting his attempt at styling it, falling down into his face instead of sweeping out of the way. I'm always surprised by how bad his acne is at this point. He has several very red spots on his nose and cheeks and chin, but his eyes are the same piercing blue I remember.

Opening the door, I walk up behind his chair and form a gun with my thumb and finger, sticking it into his back. "Not smart, letting your guard down."

He leaps up, knocking his chair over and slopping his latte all over the table. "Holy crap!" He whirls making sure his cup is upright then picks up the chair. "Who in the hell? Seeress?" His voice seems to choke on the last word, my handle.

"That's right, KnightRider. I have to say, your shiny armor sucks." I give him a dismissive appraisal before moving to the opposite seat.

He's still staring at me, standing, mouth agape.

"Heph, it's me. Sit down."

He obeys, not taking his eyes from me.

I sigh and put my chin in my hand. “Look, stop staring, okay?”

“But you’re hot.”

I can’t fight rolling my eyes. “Newsflash. I told you that.”

“Yeah, but I thought it was bullshit, like all the rest.”

“It’s not bullshit, any of it. I’ve had a lot of practice shooting, so I really am that good.”

“Yeah, right. In a range? How much practice could you have?”

I look at him blandly. “You wouldn’t believe just how many actual targets I’ve taken down.”

“Try me,” he says with a familiar cocky grin.

“Total? Seven hundred seventeen.”

“Rounds?”

“Meat sacks. Animals. Zombies. Actual threats. I’ve saved myself and others with a good shot more times than I want to remember. I’ve had a lot of practice, with a lot of different guns.”

“That I believe,” he says, leaning back in the chair. “You are ace with every weapon you pick up. Zombies? What shooter are you playing?”

"I'm not playing anything anymore. It's time to warn everyone."

He scoffs. "Warn them about what? That you're going to kick their asses?"

I clench my jaw, seconds from losing it on him. Was Heph ever this clueless before?

"Warn them that the infection that is spreading isn't a flu. It's a super virus that destroys the adult brain, rendering them mindless animals."

"How is that different from normal?" he asks glibly.

I snort. "I'm serious. Every person over the age of twenty-five is going to become a zombie in the next week or so. I want everyone under that age, that doesn't find themselves sick with their parents, to take shelter together, preferably where they can help to keep things running — power plants, gas plants, phone companies, ISPs. They aren't as safe as army barracks, but I think they can be made safe enough."

He's still staring at me like I'm mad, and I probably sound mad at the moment.

"Look," I set up the creamers from the table in a pyramid. "This is Dr. Peter Evans."

"Wasn't he the one found murdered in his toilet?"

I groan and wish Heph would focus. "Yes." I point to the top of the pyramid again. "He carries the virus home to his wife and son." I point at the two below. "They take it to the day care and the mall." I move down again. "The other kids take it home. One of their parents goes to visit her sister in Gallup." I flick one of the bottom creamers at Heph. "And the whole city gets infected."

"So, it's the flu?" he asks, looking at the tiny cup in his hands.

"No, it's much worse than the flu. It cooks their brains. They see things that aren't there, and then they can't see properly at all, all they see is food, and we're the tastiest of all."

"Brains?" he asks.

"No, well yes. They want people with brains, people who haven't changed, but they don't actually eat the brains. Well, not exclusively.

They will eat a brain, but they're just after the meat. Y' know, forget that." I'm rambling away.

"You're crazy, you know that?"

I close my eyes and try to accept that this Heph isn't going to help me. "Forget it. I'll do this myself." I push back my chair and prepare to leave. I don't want to do this without Heph, but I don't need him.

"Wait!" He reaches out and grabs my arm to stop me. "You really believe all of that?"

I sigh in exasperation. "Yes. It's going to happen. I've just delayed it, not stopped it."

"You killed Peter Evans?" He sits straighter, seeming to try to get farther from me.

"Yes, and his lab assistants, and half the employees of Manson in Albuquerque."

"You're a serial killer."

I close my eyes and start to make my way out again.

"No, wait. I believe you. Well, no, I don't, but there has to be something to it or you wouldn't do that."

"Wouldn't I?" I ask. He doesn't know me.

"No. You don't just shoot people down in the games, so you wouldn't do that in real life. You're really trying to stop the spread."

I fall heavily into my chair, weary already.

"Okay. What do you want me to do?"

"Let me know when your parents get sick. I'm going to keep watching Cory Evans. His mom hasn't turned yet. I'm going to get him out of there when she does."

"Who is Cory Evans?"

"Their son. He doesn't deserve what will happen to him if I don't snatch him when his mom gets ill, just like you didn't deserve what happened when you were grounded while your parents changed."

His eyes widened. "What did I do?"

"What you had to," I say low and quiet. "I think we're done for tonight. Check out my blog, you'll understand. Thanks for meeting me, Heph. I've missed you." I rise and hug him around the neck. He pats my back nervously. I smack his shoulder and straighten.

I post my draft blog entries, detailing the viral effects and spread as well as identifying some key infrastructure that would be good to defend. I lock myself in my car again and try to sleep, praying no meat sacks come to bang on my windows.

I'm in luck, again. How many more nights will I have? Not many, I'm sure. I'm surprised to find a text message on my phone. My friends, as they have times before, drop me when I disappear, and Heph doesn't seem to believe me yet.

It's from my mother.

Cassy, we're in the bomb shelter under the Exxon building. There is enough food and power here for three months. Don't worry about us. Keep yourself safe.

They believed me. They're safe, uninfected. Well, hopefully uninfected. If anyone inside the shelter is infected, they'll spread it to the rest. They're safe, I tell myself again.

***

Today, I plan to set up Freetown, New Mexico. Well, the first steps of it. Filling up my Taurus, I rejoice that the attendant, a woman over thirty, shows no signs of infection yet. I've bought us at least a week. In fact, I might have trouble getting people to believe me because I've held it off so well. I can't worry about that. I can only help the people closest to me.

I don't know the first thing about power plants. I don't know how to keep the power running. I do know that we won't need as much as we do now. We just need to keep it from failing altogether. If that means putting a geek in the seat for a month or two, I know a few geeks. In the meantime, my job at Manson is finished, the murders and then the infection news coming out of their offices would be enough to ruin them financially. Instead, I take a job with New Mexico's public power company. I hope to learn what I need to do before the time comes.

I keep a pistol tucked in my waistband under my shirt. This is Albuquerque and the heart of the infection. These adults could go anytime. I can see, even in my interview, that the staff are fighting the effects.

"Welcome aboard, Cassandra. I'm sure you'll . . ." the HR lady drifts off, staring in horror at something to my right.

"Maybe you should go home," I suggest as I rise from my chair. "You look like you're not feeling well."

"Yes, I could have sworn I saw......"

I hurry out of the room, fighting the urge to kill her then and there. The more meat sacks I take out ahead of time, the fewer that will come storming me later, but I can't simply shoot people in the middle of work. I don't want to end up in jail.

I shudder at that memory. On the one hand, the bars keep the cops out, but there are no supplies and no way of getting out.

The next day, Heph walks up to me in the lunchroom, fresh from HR I guess. "Well, I hope this is worth getting kicked out of the house."

I grin. "Trust me. Soon, you won't want to be at home anyway." I lean closer to him and ask, "Can't you see it?"

"What?" He looks around without shame. "That they're sick? Yeah, everyone's getting sick."

I close my eyes and curse this intelligent boy's ability to miss the obvious. "What do you think they're sick with?"

"Oh, all of them?" He starts to get up, looking very uncomfortable. "Like the pets?"

I shift nervously. I never remember the domestic animals. The humans who turn are so horrific, so quick to go after the uninfected that I forget about dogs biting children, cats pouncing dogs—all trying to devour one another. Everyone fell together before, but this time, because I've restricted the human spread, the pets went first.

"Yes."

"All of them?" he asks again.

"Yes, Heph. All of them. You, I, and maybe six other people here will be fine. The rest are either not coming to work tomorrow or the day after, or they're coming to eat us."

"No way." He shakes his head in disbelief and we start drawing attention, something I'm not keen on.

"Excuse us," I say loudly and pull Heph out of the room. "Look, learn as much as you can as fast as you can. Hopefully, we'll have a few more people to help us tomorrow. We might have to teach them what we need to keep this running. At least we'll drop down to minimal power. We only need to keep a few lines going. We'll have what we need in the building."

Heph wraps an arm around me and pulls it back as he touches the gun. "You're packing?"

"Heph, I need you, but I need you to believe me. They are going to try to eat us. We are going to have to shoot them. That's why I'm so good at those games. I've shot a lot of zombies, real ones. I'm not letting one take me by surprise because he was still acting sick."

"Oh, okay, Seeress."

"Cassy," I remind him. "That's just a handle."

“Cassy. Where can I get a gun?”

I chuckle. “I have another in my car, but we’ll want to get some rifles, too.”

“My dad has a bunch.”

“I know,” I say with a wistful sigh. “He has some nice ones. Think we can steal them?” I ask brightly.

“What?!”

I frown at this response. “Well, it’s not like he’s going to be using them. Anyway, we can just hit a camping outfitter. I’m over eighteen now.”

“You know, if we’re only keeping a few safe houses running, we probably don’t need power plants. Just generators.”

I stop dead in my tracks. “You’re right. This is stupid! What was I thinking?”

“I’m guessing you were thinking of saving the world.”

I shoot him a death glare that he pretends to ignore.

“Okay, I’m changing the web page. Where can we get old generators for cheap?”

"You're kidding, right? There's no such thing as a cheap generator."

"Well, then we need to find the easiest ones to move and we'll claim them when the time comes. In the meantime, we collect fuel."

"Diesel? Sure. You got a tanker truck?"

My eyes narrow. "No, but I bet I can find one unattended."

"You're kind of a klepto, you know?"

My eyes narrow further. "Look, in a little while everything is going to go to hell. No one will be using anything, unless it's us. So yes, I intend on taking anything we need."

"I don't think that many people look that sick."

"It gets worse fast."

Heph follows me to my car. "Nice wheels. What decade did you salvage this beast from?"

"Shut up and get in. You're going to love this car when you have to try to fix one with a computer."

He looks at the handle again. “Damn, you’re right. I can probably figure out how to do the basics on this old girl.”

“Exactly.”

We drive past a cop that’s holding one of the infected down on the ground. I roll down my window. “Just shoot him, there’s no cure.”

“I can’t do that. Now move along.”

“Your head when he bites it off,” I shout as I pull away. I don’t get far enough and hear the cop scream when the man he has cuffed takes a few fingers. I pull out my gun as I turn the corner and hit the meat sack in the head without stopping.

“Nice shot!” Heph cheers. “And ewww.”

I shrug. “One of the reasons I like rifles, I don’t have to get close.”

He nods, somber, thinking. “We’re going to kill a lot of people, aren’t we?”

“No. They won’t be people anymore when we kill them. The people will be kids, like us, and smart adults who lock themselves away, like my parents.”

“Where are your parents?”

"In a bomb shelter. I hope some others were following my blog. Mind you, if they waited this long, it's probably too late."

Heph nods beside me. "My parents, it's too late for them."

"Are they sick?"

"Yeah. Mom had a fever yesterday."

I wince. "It's not too late for your sister. Want to get her? I just have one other kid I want to snag." I pull into the Evans' driveway.

Knocking receives no answer so I open the door to find Cory in his pajamas playing in front of the TV.

"Hi, Cory. I'm Cassy. Where's your Mom?"

"Sleeping. She isn't feeling good. She gave me snacks!" He holds up the wrappers of three bite-sized fruit snacks.

I nod. "Want to go for a ride?"

"Sure!"

This kid has no sense of preservation. I love it. "Here, let's grab your booster seat," I suggest, opening the car door. Another sign of just how out-of-it Mrs. Evans is, it's unlocked. I probably got to Cory just in time.

I'm right when I hear a crashing in the house.

"Heph, get Cory belted." I close the door to the house behind me. Cory doesn't need to see this.

Mrs. Evans rushes me, jaws wide, eyes glazed. My pistol is knocked from my hand by the impact. She goes for my neck, as expected, but I roll atop her, managing to wriggle my knife out of my pocket. I slit her throat and then her eyes. Blind, she's a lot less effective. It's gross and worse than a kill, but this knife isn't going to decapitate a cat. I push away from her flailing hands and get the gun back. The bullet does what my knife couldn't. Looking down, I take a moment to judge Mrs. Evans' size. We're probably close enough. Jogging up the stairs, I swap my now bloody t-shirt and shorts for a loose sundress from her closet.

"That's Mom's!" Cory says with glee.

"Yeah, she's letting me borrow it. Pretty?"

"Pretty!" he agrees.

"Beautiful," Heph murmurs.

"Aw, thanks." I lean over and give him a peck, which startles him. Rather than say anything, I back out of the drive. "Umm, Heph, you and I...this isn't the first time I've gone to you for help."

"I've never met you before, Seeress."

"You haven't, but I have. This is the fifth time I've done all this, Heph. With the exception of the last time, when Cory and I went on a vacation, I always come to you." I check on the kid. He's asleep. "You taught me how to shoot, how to fight. You taught me how to play those stupid games on the computer."

"We had sex?!"

It never fails to amaze me how linear Heph's thought pattern is.

"Yes. A few times. You got me knocked up once."

"Shit. I don't want to do that."

I can't help it, I laugh loudly enough to wake Cory.

"Sorry, kid. You okay back there?"

"I need to pee."

I slam the brakes and pull over. Heph braces on the dash. "What the hell?!"

I'm already unstrapping my belt and opening Cory's door. "He doesn't mess around about going pee."

"Here?" Cory asks.

"Yep. Leave the door open and I'll stand on this side." As if he's modest. He's just looking for an excuse, I think.

"Okay." There's a bit of dribbling and I help him back into the booster seat. "Now I'm thirsty," he says as soon as I snap the belt.

"Of course you are," I say with a smile. "Can you wait a few miles? It's not far to my house."

"O—kay." He drags the word out.

"Are we really going to your house?" Heph asks as I merge back into traffic.

"Yep. My parents are holed up in a bomb shelter, so it's safe enough. We can eat what's left in the cupboards until it's time to found Freetown."

"That's kind of a lame name."

I punch him in the bicep.

"Ow. Well, it is."

"Tell the cadets at Fort Carson. They named the first one."

"Cassy?"

"Yes, Heph?"

"Are you going to treat me like a sidekick?"

"Only until you man up enough to be the hero."

He sets his jaw. "What does that mean?"

"You won't have to fight your way out of your house this time. That means you need something else to convince you that this is real, that lives are on the line, that you can save them. I couldn't convince you of that the second time; you were never my Heph."

He's quiet after that and the car is filled with the sounds of Cory singing the theme song to one of his cartoons.

"I want to be your Heph."

I smile, lean over, and kiss him quickly. "I do, too."

CHAPTER FOURTEEN

WE'RE SUCCESSFUL. Freetown, New Mexico is set up near my parents' bomb shelter. The best part about this time, the fifth time, the last time, is that I can write letters to them and receive letters from them. When they take the books and supplies we leave outside for them, they leave letters for us in their place.

Using the last of the Internet and cell service, we find out about other liberated pockets all over the country. None is larger than a couple thousand kids, the ones that escaped—small towns, no cities, none in the US anyway. Japan has a huge colony of kids in Tokyo who are claiming to have eliminated every adult in the city. I'm doubtful, but wish them luck. They also claim to have found every survivor in their country—I find that ridiculous.

There isn't really a way to keep in touch with the other pockets, but I find my favorite people. Kenny is in still in Colorado. Jenny is herding youngsters in Texas. Their equivalents are here. Jordan is our science buff. Melanie looks after all the little ones. Jordan doesn't have Ken's medical background and Melanie isn't pregnant, but I still think of them as Ken and Jenny sometimes, missing the real thing.

Cory is great. He's one of the youngest kids in the complex. There's a little girl who's three, but she's the only one younger than him. He and Trix are inseparable, constantly coloring, sculpting, making mud pies or pillow forts together. It makes me glad we took a penitentiary. It has a great courtyard that is completely safe.

Melanie lacks Jenny's green thumb, but a girl named Lily has broken ground for a garden. With a name like that, I expect great things; we get them. Early in the spring she starts planting. The spring, who would have thought I would make it to March? It's only a few days away. I take that as the ultimate sign that this really is the last time.

There is one big change, one that makes me worry for Trix and Cory. More kids are getting sick, always the oldest, but almost randomly. If Kenny was right, they've gotten old enough that their hormones aren't fighting off the virus anymore. It's scary to think the little ones might be left alone.

We're still trying to find the few isolated individuals that didn't make it to one of the safe compounds, although we have less hope with each passing week. At some point, we'll abandon the searches; anyone surviving this long has their own safe house. Heph is leading the groups from our Freetown. Just like the first time, he is driven to save people. He and I, as well as a couple other pairs, head out every few weeks. We go as far as we can on a tank, and then turn around and come back. Each trip is treacherous. The meat sacks converge at the scent of fresh meat, making me wonder how anyone can survive out there. There doesn't seem to be a mammal left that isn't feeding on one another.

"I still think we should call it Liberton."

"Heph, the city has a name. We could always call it Albuquerque again."

"No way. That name sucks worse than Freetown. Who got happy with the q anyway?"

I laugh, having no answer. My head is bothering me and I wipe sweat off my brow.

"Is it warm for March?" Part of me is giddy that it is March. I've never made it this far.

"I don't think so. I mean, it's not cold, but I don't think it's warm."

"Just me then." I shrug and watch the road, laying down cover fire when a new pack of meat sacks rush the van. "Heph, flag at three o'clock."

He turns the van to the right and we aim for the courthouse, the only building in town with a flag. Not something the meat sacks would put up and normally it should have blown away or been ripped up, but it looks like it's in good shape. It's not the first time something like a flag or a message spray painted on a building lets us know someone is inside.

We both unload a few rounds to clear a path to the door, then I hold the stairs as Heph makes his way inside. It isn't warm, and I can feel a breath of winter still clinging, reminding me of the first time. This was exactly how I died. Only I didn't have ammunition, so I was fighting with blades. This time I have paired semi-automatics. I feel a lot more secure.

Sweat prickles on my brow. Didn't I just think there was a chill in the air? Why am I sweating? I unload on a new pack of sacks, five of them mowed down by my bullets. Usually seeing one go down intimidates the rest, but another will always come.

I've been keeping my back to the door, knowing that's safest, but I whirl at something just out of sight on my right. I fire without thought, planning to shoot it down. It turns out to only be a reflection off a car.

Blinking and shaking my head, I put my back to the door again just before a new wave of meat sacks come out of an alley.

"Hurry it up, Heph," I say through clenched teeth, taking these down as well. Then I shiver. What is wrong with me? Have I caught a cold? I can't remember the last time anyone in Freetown had a cold.

This time the movement in my periphery is on the left and again I spin without thought, exposing my back. Firing both pistols on automatic, I shred a mailbox to scrap.

Squinting, blinking, I try to figure out what I'd been shooting at. I hear a roar followed by more shots. Heph's back is to mine.

"What are you doing, Cassy?"

I shake my head to clear it. "I don't know. I thought I saw something."

"This group is all girls, no guns. They keep locking themselves in different buildings, hoping to throw them off the scent."

"That can't work."

"No, they've lost half their number, but we can take these six back with us."

Only six. Well, every one counts.

I wipe my forehead again, slick with sweat. Then I unzip my jacket and put one of my pistols back in its holster.

"What are you doing?!" Heph asks, astounded. "Keep that out. We need to get back on the road."

I pull it out quickly. "Right, sorry. Let's go."

The girls cluster between Heph and I as we hustle them toward the van. As soon as we reach it, I open the door for them to pile in and take out the jerry can to refill the tank. Heph keeps his eye on the street, watching in both directions. He only has to fire a few times.

I'm just setting the can down when I see something just behind the van, peeking around the corner. I drop the can, letting the remaining gasoline slop out and pull my gun to shoot.

"Cassy!" Heph yells. "Get in the van."

I obey, reluctantly, keeping my gun trained on the flash of red just out of sight.

Heph throws the can in to the girls. “Close that.”

I make my way into the drivers’ seat, wiping my forehead again. My stomach isn’t feeling good anymore either. Something is definitely wrong. I blink my eyes to try to clear them.

“You okay? You don’t look so good. Something wrong? Did you know one of them?” He jerks his head at the carnage we’ve left behind us.

“No, not that. Just sick, I guess, probably from all this cold weather. I told you we should have taken south.”

He laughs. “We totally lost out on south. You’re lucky we didn’t get north.”

I shudder again, only half at the thought of my warm southwest bones going into the frozen reaches of Wyoming, or worse, Montana. I wonder if any Canadians survived. How are they doing?

I shiver again.

“You okay to drive?” Heph asks.

“Yeah, I’ll be fine.” A meat sack jumps out in front of the van like an idiot, and I run him down. The girls are sobbing in the back, and it makes my headache even worse. I start to have an inkling of what’s wrong with me, but I refuse to admit it. Instead, I give Heph a look of weariness. He grins and turns to look over his shoulder.

“It’s okay,” Heph assures them. “It’s over now. We’re taking you somewhere they can’t reach. We’re taking you somewhere we’re free.”

His speech works as it does every time. It helps that his acne has cleared and his five-o’clock shadow makes him look rugged. It doesn’t help that he’s still a geek; my geek, my badass. He found something in this horror to turn him into the hero from the sidekick. We’re definitely partners now and today, at least, he’s carrying the brunt of the load.

The drive is long and we have to stop to refill the tank. We’re going to run out of gasoline soon. Jordan had better get the solar and wind power running in Freetown ASAP. We’re going to need all the fuel for vehicles, not generators. I know

Jordan is close to getting it up, but for some reason the details are fuzzy. This can't be happening to me.

I'm shivering nonstop as we pull into the gate. Three kids come out to open the fence for us. There is no rush of meat sacks here. There are very few left in the area. I wish that meant I could let my parents out of their self-imposed prison, but we're still carrying the virus, as exemplified by my symptoms.

"We're home, Cassy. We made it." Speaking of self-imprisonment, the outside of the pen doesn't look any better than when it housed convicts. At least we've been able to make the inside better. Raids have gotten curtains and proper doors for all the cells, giving us perfect apartments for sleeping. Heph wants to share mine, and I want him to join me, but there's still a little something holding us apart. I wish more than ever that I'd just told him to stay with me.

Heph kisses me, a quick peck. He frowns and kisses my forehead. "You're burning up. Let's get you inside."

The more I think about my symptoms, the more I see things out of the corner of my eye, the more I can't deny what's wrong. I defined these symptoms, after all.

"I'm not going inside, Heph." I leave the keys in the ignition and slide out of the seat to the ground. I hold the vinyl for a minute while the world spins and images dance everywhere. My vision is starting to swim and it feels like my brain is melting. My body is cold, but my head is burning. I know what this is. I didn't think it was possible, but I'm changing. It's only a matter of time until my brain is mush and I'm looking for someone to eat. I can't give up. This is the last time. That means there must be something for me out there, something I need to learn as a meat sack.

"Take the girls. I'm headed that way." I point randomly away. "If I can survive this, I will. Take care of them. Take care of yourself. When did you get wings?" I can see them now, shining out of his back, glowing around him. "And don't cry. You never cry." It's true. Even when he killed his own parents, every time he told me what it was like, he didn't cry, but there are tears in his eyes now, a look of pity.

He kisses me again, longer this time. His tongue feels cold against the heat in my mouth, but it is so familiar, so comforting. I indulge, letting the heat in my blood boil with his touch. I wish the girls weren't here so I could spend these last minutes alone with Heph. Still, even just a kiss makes this a little easier. I push him away and turn to run.

I'm not giving up. This is the last time. I don't know what being a meat sack is like. Maybe I can hold onto something they can't. If I can, I can find a way to pull all the sacks away from the Freetowns of the world. Could I do that?

Something red in the distance pulls my eye. It must be a delusion. It looks like an ant that is bigger than me.

"Good bye, Cassy," Heph says.

A moment later a bullet passes through my head. My brain is already melted enough that I feel it, but it doesn't kill me immediately. The remainder works for a few moments, making me breathe, making my legs thrash. I remember my parents, that they're safe, and then the remainder of my grey and white matter can't pass messages at all and my lungs stop. I'm aware and pain-free for another minute while my lungs cease to breathe, my heart doesn't pump. The ant-thing is standing over me—stupid delusions—touching my head with an odd claw as I die.

CHAPTER FIFTEEN

I SHIVER uncontrollably in the shallow salt water, hugging myself. I never thought I could be turned. That was never a possibility, or Heph shooting me. I shudder again, tears streaming my cheeks. My stomach turns at the memory, and I lean to one side, retching in the surf.

I wipe my mouth and rise, tying my hair in a knot. I don't have time to waste. This is the last time. I know the cause. I know how to stop it.

"Mom, Dad. I'm not feeling well. Would you mind heading back early?" I ask as I approach them. They heard me retching so the excuse is really believable.

"Sure, sweetie," my mom says, touching my face. "Something you ate?"

"Yeah, I think so. Too much sun?"

"That would make sense," my dad agrees, unlocking the Caravan. "Let's get you home."

As soon as I'm up in my room, I open the window and climb out. I have the keys for the Taurus in my pocket and Mom and Dad are in the wrong part of the house to hear me peel away. I should be in Albuquerque in an hour, just as the cleaning staff starts their shift. Jane will be working tonight. I remember her shift from last time.

Pulling into the staff lot, I make my way to the ladies locker room. Jane is just loading her cart. She is startled to see me, but doesn't get out more than a squeak before I put her in a choke hold.

"I'm sorry, Jane. I just need your pass for the night, just a couple of hours. You'll be fine here."

We both slide to ground as she becomes dead weight in my arms. I lay her on her side and yank the badge from her uniform. Then I pull on a matching uniform from the pile of laundry and hurry for the elevator.

“Come on. Come on.” I chant as the metal box climbs ten floors to Evans’ lab. Every moment is one more replication of the virus.

I dash out as soon as the door opens and nearly crash into Evans. “Oh! I’m sorry, Doctor. I didn’t think anyone was still here.” I keep my eyes down, like a good cleaning lady.

“I’m the last. Follow your instructions,” he reminds me.

“Yes, doctor. I won’t touch anything.” A total lie. I’m going to touch everything.

“Good night, Jane.”

Thank God I look a little like Jane, especially with my hair in this ponytail. “Good night, Doctor.” I pass him, using Jane’s badge to open the door. This is perfect. If I remember the records I read last time, the fifth time, he’ll have injected either the rabbits or the rats just before he left. I run to the cage and pull out the first one.

I have a moment of pity for the rabbit. I pat his long white ears. “I’m sorry. I can’t let you eat your friends, and I can’t let you spread what you carry.” I snap the tiny neck in a series of quick pops. I stroke each of the other five the same way before doing the same with the rats. I even kiss a couple. Such innocent creatures, but now capable of such destruction.

I toss the carcasses into the chute to the incinerator and start looking for any notes. I find several hand-written lab results and toss them in after the rabbits. I throw every test tube, every beaker, every container holding any liquid down the same chute. I erase every white board. Finally, I go to the computers with plans to wipe the drives, just like Heph taught me a long time ago, the first time. He warned that there’ll always be a chance of recovery, but there’s a chance of off-site backups too. I can only do so much. The best thing I can do is warn Dr. Evans. I’m glad I don’t have to kill him. Cory deserves a dad.

Dr. Evans,

You made a terrible mistake. Please do not make your virus airborne in the future.

Setting the note in the center of the now empty table, I turn back to the door and key in a quarantine. The room will be sealed for the next twenty-four hours. Any virus still in the air will be dead unless it finds a living host.

I pick up a scalpel from the table and stretch my arm over one of the sinks. The only living creature bearing the virus now is me. The idea of suicide is repugnant, but if I've made a mistake, I should just jump back to the beach, right? I've never done this though, never taken my own life.

"Wait!"

I turn quickly and knock an empty beaker off the drying rack. It stops halfway to the ground. I can't help but stare at it. Then I stare at the person in the locked room with me. Is it a person? The voice was vaguely feminine but the body is completely foreign to me, like a giant ant. Huge eyes point in opposite directions on the top of her bright red head and two lips are turned the wrong way, vertically, under a slit of a nose. I recognize the figure, but I'd sworn she was a delusion.

"Cassandra. You never gave up before, why start now?"

"Who...What are you?"

"I'm a time traveler. By the rules of my people, I couldn't stop this disaster. I'm not allowed to do anything. However, I could help you stop it. You could change things. You did change things. I could send you back because you refused to accept death, refused to believe it was the end, even when you were infected yourself. I thought we'd lost that time. You can set that back on the rack if you like." She lifts an odd red claw, her hand, to point to the beaker.

I do as she suggests.

The room seems to get marginally lighter and the door unlocks with a thunk. Looking at the clock on the wall, I see it is a few minutes earlier. "You can go," she tells me. "You weren't infected. It was still incubating. You won't spread it. You did it, Cassy. You closed the loop."

“Wait.” I hold up my hands and turn to the pair of wiped computers. Opening the cases I pull out hard drives and ram chips, pocketing the lot. No chance of recovery now. “Still won’t stop off-site backups.”

The time traveler laughs. It’s an odd clicking, but definitely happy sounding. “Oh, I think they’ll find when they go for their backups, they are corrupted.”

“Nice!” I stop at my note. Picking up the pen, I add a signature.

Sincerely,

Mankind.

“I figured I didn’t need to sign it when they were going to find me here.”

“But now they won’t!” the time traveler finishes with another odd laugh. “Oh, one more thing, Cassandra,” she says as I open the door. “This means the next time you die, you’ll really die.”

“Best news I’ve heard all day,” I answer honestly. I can live my life. I can do whatever I want with the rest of my summer. Maybe I actually will work in Mr. Brown's ice cream shop. I've gotten to like kids after living with so many. I can meet Heph slowly, by chance. Well, when he isn't grounded anymore.

"Say, do you know why Heph is grounded?"

The time traveler makes an odd hum. "No. I'm afraid I was only watching you."

I shrug. "It's between us anyway." Then a sadness fills me. My Heph was a construction of the disaster. Will anything happen now to turn him into the hero I knew, the protector? Maybe. Maybe not. I don't have to rush. We can be friends for years. I don't need a boyfriend, such a big change from the first time. What will Julie say when I tell her that? I don't really care. I'm not likely to keep in touch with my most vapid friends as we head for colleges, although I will have my birthday party. One last hurrah, end of high school, end of life as a child and time to be one of the adults. I'm not afraid.

As the elevator doors close behind me, I let out a squeal and jump in the air. I'm not an adult yet and this time I really did it. This time, the last time, I stopped the damn thing.

THE END

About The Author

Kimberly Gould hates being called Kimmy, but her mother called her Kimmydonn and that was okay. She lives in Edmonton, Alberta with her husband and daughter. When she isn't writing about the post-apocalyptic world, she is doing her best to prevent an apocalypse as an environmental consultant. You can find her anywhere online as Kimmydonn including her website, kimmydonn.com

Proof

67074437R00197

Made in the USA
Charleston, SC
03 February 2017